The
TWISTED
TREE

The Twisted Tree

RACHEL BURGE

HOT KEY
BOOKS

First published in Great Britain in 2019 by
HOT KEY BOOKS
80–81 Wimpole St, London W1G 9RE
www.hotkeybooks.com

A CIP catalogue record for this book is available from the British Library.

ISBN: 978-1-4714-0776-5
also available as an ebook

3

Typeset by Palimpsest Book Production Ltd, Falkirk, Stirlingshire
Printed and bound in Great Britain by Clays Ltd, Elcograf S.p.A.

Hot Key Books is an imprint of Bonnier Books UK
www.bonnierbooks.co.uk

*This book is dedicated to Odin,
inspirer of poets; god of wisdom,
magic and sacrifice.*

MARTHA — 24 JANUARY

*I*t started the day I fell from the tree at Mormor's cabin in Norway. The day I became blind in one eye.

I'm going to write it all down here, no matter how crazy it makes me sound. If I have a daughter one day, she deserves to know the truth –

The truth.

Why couldn't Mum have just told me? The thought is like a knot in my brain, and the more I pick, the tighter it gets. If I had known, I could have done something and no one would have died. If she had told me, the horror of these past few days might never have happened.

THE STAIN OF A SOUL

My stomach shrinks to a hard ball as we pull into Heathrow. The platform is heaving with people. Holding my rucksack in front of me, I grit my teeth and push my way through the crowd. As people brush past me I get flashes of their lives – their memories and emotions – but it happens so fast I can't make sense of it.

My hands are sweaty as I pull my phone from my pocket. I check the time, then wish I hadn't. Last check-in is in fifteen minutes. I *can't* miss this flight.

A train pulls into the platform opposite and dozens of passengers spill out. Worried their clothes will touch me, I veer left and head for the escalator. A man passes me, coming up the other way, and for a horrible moment I think it's Dad, but it's just some other grey businessman.

Inside the departure hall people rush around me, dragging reluctant suitcases and even more reluctant children. The noise is like a swarm of bees, all wanting to sting me. It's not just the hubbub of conversation. The air sparks and crackles – it's like their clothes *know* I'm here, walking among them.

A wet-faced toddler wobbles in my direction, hands outstretched, closely followed by a tired-looking woman. I swerve but not quickly enough to avoid her brushing my arm. The woman had five miscarriages before she had her daughter. She's pregnant again but lies awake at night, terrified she might lose this baby too. My chest aches with emptiness, her loss so sharp it makes me catch my breath. I walk away, then glance back at her red coat. I've been through Mum's wardrobe enough times in the past few months to know it must be at least fifty-per-cent cashmere. Wool holds a person's emotions but cashmere is different – it makes you feel them.

Spotting the familiar sign for Scandinavian Airlines, I head towards the check-in desk, then stumble over a suitcase and nearly go flying.

'Hey! Watch it!' a man snaps.

'Sorry. I didn't see. Sorry,' I mumble.

'It might help if you took off your sunglasses!'

I join the back of the queue, my face burning with embarrassment. Being blind in one eye messes with your depth perception. I can't work out distances; when

I focus on something in the foreground it makes stuff in the distance go blurry. It wasn't a problem at home because I know where everything is, but now . . . if I can't even make it across the airport without falling over, how am I going to make it to Norway?

I hold the silver charm around my neck and tell myself to get it together. I've done the journey with Mum lots of times, and I had no problem travelling around London by myself before the accident. I just need to focus.

There are two families ahead of me; if they're quick maybe I can still make my flight. I rummage through my bag and pull out my printed e-ticket and ferry pass to Skjebne. You pronounce it *Sheb-na* – heavy on the Shh, which is kind of fitting, as it turns out. We used to spend every summer there – Dad too before he left us – but since the accident Mum refuses to talk about the island or Mormor, my grandma.

'Next customer, please.'

I step forward and lay my passport and e-ticket on the desk.

'Where are you travelling to today, miss?'

'Bodø. Well, Skjebne, actually. But I have to change flights at Oslo and then get the ferry from Bodø. And it's Martha Hopkins. My name, that is.' My face reddens. I sound like such an idiot.

As I put my rucksack on the scales, the woman behind the desk leans over and whispers to her colleague before turning back to me. I stare at my feet, convinced she can tell I'm a runaway just by looking at me.

'Can you remove your sunglasses, please?'

My voice is as shaky as my legs. 'Why? Is there a problem?'

'I need to verify you're the person shown in the passport photo.' She glances behind me. 'Travelling alone? No parent or guardian?'

'No, but I'm seventeen and your website said –'

'The picture in this passport shows a much younger child.'

I bite my thumbnail as she slides my passport across the desk, open at the page with my photo, as if I don't already know what it looks like. I glance at the image of the pale-faced girl with long blonde hair and quickly look away. I hate seeing pictures of me from before.

'I've always been small for my age,' I blurt, then instantly feel stupid.

She studies the photo and I clutch my necklace. Most of the jewellery I made after the accident was rubbish, yet this piece came out perfectly. The feel of its cool edges always calms me. I love metal; it tells me nothing.

I take a deep breath. 'Look, I'm actually late. So if you could –'

'Take off your glasses, miss.'

Somebody behind me tuts. I snatch off my shades and stare at the woman, or rather my right eye does. My left eye is looking who knows where. Her eyes widen, then flick down to my passport. 'Thank you. A last call was put out for your flight five minutes ago. You'll have to be quick. Gate 33 – up the escalator and to your left.'

I shove my glasses back on with a trembling hand and turn away, but not quick enough to avoid seeing her pity smile. I don't have to touch her clothes to know what she's thinking. Her thoughts are written all over her face: poor girl, how terrible, she would be pretty too, if it weren't for that. A patronising look and then she moves on, anxious to lay eyes on someone who doesn't look like a freak.

At the top of the escalator I go through security, where I have to take off my sunglasses and necklace again. Thankfully people are too busy patting their pockets for loose change that isn't there to notice my face. Once I'm through the metal detector, I snatch my stuff from the plastic tray, replace my shades and hurry to my boarding gate.

An air stewardess wearing a jaunty blue hat looks at my pass and shakes her head.

My heart lurches. 'Please. I *really* need to get this flight.'

She takes in my trainers. 'You can run?' I grin and she ushers me onto the connecting air bridge and we rush to the end. When we get to the plane I put my necklace on, grateful to feel its cool silence against my skin.

Everyone is seated, ready for take-off. I walk along the aisle, searching for my place. Boarding the plane was always the most exciting part of the journey when I was little. Now the thought of being crammed in a box with strangers makes me feel sick. I look at the people around me: a white fur coat bristling with outrage; a chunky knit heavy with sorrow. I can't tell what secrets they hold just by looking at them, but it's hard to stop my imagination sometimes.

I find my row and my heart sinks. There's a huge man next to the aisle, and my seat is by the window. Brian – according to the stretched name on his rugby shirt – is wearing earphones, and his eyes are closed.

'Excuse me, I need to get in.'

No response.

A flight attendant is heading this way, folding up tray tables and opening blinds with the determination of a trained assassin. I raise my voice, but Brian doesn't hear. The normal thing would be to touch his shoulder, but I don't want his rugby shirt to speak to me. Maybe I should prod his hand. In the end I pull down his tray table, bashing it against his knees. He jumps awake and grumbles, then stands to let me pass.

I smile a thank-you, then stash my coat and try to make myself as small as possible. Luckily my own clothes tell me nothing. I guess it's like the way you can't smell your own scent.

My phone bleeps: a message from Mum asking if I've arrived at Dad's. I text back straight away, then turn my phone to flight mode. My parents have barely spoken since the divorce; as long as I reply, there should be no reason for her to call Dad.

The plane speeds up and I feel myself pushed back into the seat as the ground rumbles beneath me.

Suddenly Brian's elbow nudges mine. An onslaught of facts washes over me – they come so fast and hard I can barely keep up with them. His mother would lock him in a room as a child. Some nights he dreams he's still there, crying for his mummy. My breath catches. Anger, fear, rejection. They come at me in waves.

I flinch, then rub my head and try to make sense of the jumbled impressions in my brain. His rugby top must be made of polyester. Man-made fibres don't breathe; they throw things at you like a sobbing toddler too distraught to come up for air.

The world tips away beneath me and my stomach turns. I close my eyes until I feel the plane level off. When I look out of the window there is nothing but pale empty blue. The light bouncing off the wing of the plane is brilliant white – too pure, almost.

I close my eyes and instantly I'm back in hospital: waking up to blackness. Just remembering the feel of the bandages on my face makes me shudder. Maybe it was the shock, but after I came round, I couldn't stop shivering. Mum draped her jacket around my shoulders and then . . . even now I can't explain. Something wrenched apart inside me, as if a gust of wind had banged a door open. I saw myself under the tree, my blonde hair caked with blood, and then I felt a rush of emotion: fear mixed with guilt and love. Feelings that I knew weren't mine.

At first I was convinced I must have imagined it – until it happened again. After the operation they weren't sure how much of my sight had been saved.

When the doctor unfurled the bandages from my eyes, his jacket sleeve brushed my cheek. As soon as the material touched me, I saw an image of a bearded man in a reflection on a hearse window, his face pale and drawn. The man's father had died and left everything to his new wife. My heart twisted with jealousy. I could almost taste the bitterness he felt. The doctor removed the last of my bandages and I blinked in disbelief – he was the man I had seen.

That night I lay awake, terrified I was losing my mind. I told myself I must have been hallucinating, even though deep down I knew it was real. The hospital psychiatrist came to see me, concerned how I was coping with my disfigured face, but I didn't tell him anything. If he knew I can tell a person's secrets just by touching their clothes, I wouldn't be on a plane right now. I'd be listening to the ramblings of a strait-jacket.

Brian takes out a book and cracks open the spine. Anyone who does that is not a good person as far as I'm concerned. It's up there with cruelty to kittens and nose-picking in public. Yet I can't help feeling sorry for him. If I touched his top again, maybe I could offer him some words of comfort. Something tells me his mother couldn't help the way she was. I'm sure lots of mental illnesses went undetected in previous generations; nowadays she would be given medication. Like Mum.

Thinking about Mum makes my head pound. I turn my shoulder to Brian and snap the blind shut. His life is none of my business, and besides, what can I say that will make a difference? The past will always haunt him. Pain like that stays with you; it seeps out of your pores and into the fibres of your clothes, and nothing can remove the stain of a soul.

No Bullet Can Stop the Dead

Wearing dark shades at night is a risky strategy, even if your eyesight is normal. People won't see my horrible eye, but bouncing off walls and stumbling over toddlers is pretty much guaranteed to draw attention. Luckily Bodø ferry terminal is brightly lit. Not that I have to worry. Apart from the woman behind the kiosk across the hall, I'm the only one here.

I unscrew the cap of my Coke and the fizz sounds weirdly loud. There's something creepy about busy places when they're deserted, like a school at night with rows of empty desks, or a fairground with no blaring lights or music.

When we came before, Mum used to pick up a rental car from Bodø airport and drive us onto the vehicle ferry. At least being on foot means I can get the express boat. Just as well – I'm going to be knackered by the time I get there.

Suddenly it hits me. How can I have been so stupid? Mum isn't here to drive me from the harbour to Mormor's. Even if there was a taxi service on the island, which there isn't, I couldn't afford it. When we get to Skjebne I've got a long walk ahead of me – in the dark. Too late now. I haven't got the money to go back even if I wanted.

My phone bleeps with a text from Kelly. *What time you getting here hun? Hope you've got something sexy to wear, Darren is coming x*

The party! I'd forgotten. I hate missing out, but then Kelly's cousin Darren is the last person I want to see my face. I've been flirting with him on and off for about a year. We kissed at her last birthday party, and I always thought . . . Well, it doesn't matter what I thought.

I text back: *Sorry Kels can't make it. On way to see Mormor. Was a last minute thing. Waiting for ferry now!*

I feel bad for letting Kelly down, but I was always planning to make some excuse and bail. She thinks it's because of how I look, but it's not just that. I can't face being in a room with lots of people. I've tried wearing gloves but it makes no difference; people's clothes only have to brush mine for me to know their secrets.

My fingers grip my phone so hard my knuckles turn white. I can't even go to my best friend's party! If I don't get rid of this thing, how am I ever going to go to university or have a life? Being able to tell things about people seems like this amazing gift, but it's not. Not when I can't control the flood of emotions I get. Knowing someone's secrets doesn't make you feel closer to them – it pushes you away. There are some things you don't want to know, trust me.

My phone bleeps: *What?! Is that a good idea? Text when u arrive. Worried about u x*

I sigh and drop my phone on the table. Kelly is just like Mum. She thinks I should stop hiding in my room and go back to school. They want me to forget about the accident and move on – but they don't understand. I told Kelly about my weird ability once. She hugged me and said she believed me, but her raincoat was so full of doubt I could practically feel the disbelief dripping from it. After that, I kept it to myself.

I glance around the deserted terminal and shiver, feeling suddenly alone. I take out my wallet and flick through the colourful foreign notes: I have 100 NOK left, less than a tenner. Echoes mock my steps as I cross the hall. When I get to the kiosk, the assistant's head snaps up like the dead waking. I spend the last of my money on chocolate cookies – one dark and one white. My grandma has a terrible sweet tooth; we can celebrate my arrival by eating them together.

Before me, blue ropes mark the winding path to the exit. Silly to walk miles for no reason. I shove my rucksack under and duck after it. It feels a little bit wrong, even though there's no one to queue. Blowing my last dime on cookies *and* bucking the system. I can almost hear what Kelly would say: *You need to get out more, girl.*

I touch the charm around my neck and feel bad for being cross with her. I know she cares about me. Kelly wears her heart on her sleeve – and unlike some people, I don't have to touch her clothes to know she loves me.

'Eie du ingen skam?' calls a voice. This time it's not just the kiosk assistant who startles. Three teenage boys appear behind me, laughing. They're older than me by a couple of years. One of them holds a can of beer. Tall with fair hair, freckles and white teeth – a typical good-looking island boy. I carry on walking and he calls again. *'Ingen skam!'* I have no idea what it means, but he's so cute I can't help smiling.

When I get to the exit doors, I glance back. The boy is sprawled across a seat, chatting to his friends. He raises his beer in a friendly gesture and I half smile, then turn away, my face hot. I'm rubbish with boys, never mind ones that speak a different language. Besides, he's hardly going to be interested in me.

Outside, the night air is so cold it takes my breath away. A razor-sharp wind cuts into my face and blows my hair about, tugging me in every direction. I head towards the ferry and rub my arms with relief – I'll soon be at Mormor's. She might pretend to tell me off, but I know she'll be pleased I came. The thought of seeing her warms my insides. My grandma gives the best hugs.

'*Hei, fina!*' The boy again. I walk a little quicker but don't turn around. There's no one else. He must be shouting at me. A few more steps to the boat and I can hide inside.

Ouch.

Something slams against my leg. A metal post. I wince and rub my thigh. Definitely too dark for sunglasses. I snatch them off, annoyed, but without them I feel naked.

'*Hei!* Beautiful girl!' A hand on my shoulder. The boy jumps in front of me, his beer sloshing out on the wooden walkway. His grin vanishes, replaced by a look of horror, quickly followed by embarrassment. He throws up his hands and backs away. 'Sorry, sorry!' His friends see my face and howl with laughter.

I stand frozen to the spot and watch as they jostle each other onto the ferry. Is this what my life is going to be like now? Once the boys have boarded, I hurry towards the boat, the metal gangplank bouncing under my feet. At the top, I hold the door to steady myself and quickly step aboard.

I look for a dark corner where I can curl up and die, but raucous laughter from the bar persuades me to brave the upper deck. Even if it's not well lit, there probably won't be many people to stare. I grab the metal handrail and climb the steep stairway. Footsteps sound behind me. My pulse quickens. They're too close, gaining on me.

'*Hei?*'

I turn and see a tall man with a bushy grey beard.

He looks familiar, but I can't place him. His weather-worn face crinkles into a smile as he jabs a thumb to his chest. 'Olav.'

Relief washes over me. He lives on a farm a few miles from Mormor. I barely know him, but it's wonderful to see someone I recognise.

He follows me up the remaining steps and stands next to me on deck. In his hand is a long metal box, the kind that holds a snooker cue or a rifle. We haven't spoken before, though Mormor often chatted to him on our walks. He looks different: older and more stooped.

'*Ja*, det e dæ. Marta!'

He says my name the Norwegian way, and speaks in the lilting, sing-song cadence I know so well – an accent Mormor shares but Mum has pretty much lost.

I smile awkwardly and pull a strand of hair from my mouth. He says something, but the wind yanks my hood over my head and I can't hear. 'Sorry, what?'

He points at my face. '*Ditt øye?*' I don't know if Mormor told him about the accident. She never came to the hospital – not that I'm surprised; I don't think she's ever left the island, and we flew straight home to London afterwards. I haven't seen or spoken to her since.

I shrug, feeling glad when Olav leaves it at that. We stand in silence, watching the twinkling lights of the shoreline get smaller as the ferry pulls away.

He strokes his beard, then peers around me as if

17

expecting to see someone. 'Why no . . . ?' When I don't answer, he rubs a thumb across his lip. 'Ja.' He says it the way all Norwegians do, on the in-breath. I wish I could help, but my Norwegian is worse than his English. He frowns and asks something about Mormor, but falls silent when I don't understand.

Holding the rail with both hands, I lean over and lick the salt-tang of the sea from my lips. The ferry pitches from side to side as it bounces through the waves. I like the feeling. The faster we go, the sooner I'll get to Skjebne.

Olav raises a finger to indicate he'll be back. He points to the metal case at my feet and I nod to say I'll look after it. There are a few couples on deck but no one close by. I gaze in wonder at the glorious full moon and sparkling sea. The night is so wild and free and full of possibility I want to drink it in.

A seagull cries overhead and I think about the last time I saw Mormor. She took me out to the tree the day before the accident, then gave me her gloves to hold and told me to listen. I tried, but all I could hear was the lonely cry of a gull.

'Keep trying, my child, and one day you will hear,' she said. When I asked *what* I would hear, she wouldn't tell me. She had done the same thing when I was younger. Took me to the tree, put her shawl around me and told me to listen.

I think about all the letters I've written her in the last few months, asking the same question over and over: why can I tell things about people by touching their clothes? I was so worried when she didn't write back, I thought she must be sick or that she'd had an accident. Mormor doesn't have a phone, so I begged Mum to call someone on the island and ask them to check on her. Mum told me not to worry; Skjebne often has problems with its postal service. I actually believed her – until I touched her silk blouse. Mum put her arm around me to comfort me, and I saw an image of her hands burning an envelope at the kitchen sink.

Mum had bought the blouse a few days ago, and it was the first time I'd touched silk. I know from going through her wardrobe that different types of fabric reveal their secrets differently – cashmere holds a person's emotions and makes you feel them like your own; cotton shows images and facts without feeling – but silk is like nothing else. It speaks of deceit.

I rub my head, angry with myself for not figuring out Mum's lies sooner. Olav reappears clutching two polystyrene cups and two *Kvikk Lunsj*. I recognise the striped red, yellow and green packaging instantly: the Norwegian version of Kit-Kat. He gestures for me to help myself and I take the cup and chocolate with a smile. The coffee is hot with no milk or cream to dilute it.

Olav sips, stroking his beard. When he thinks I'm not looking, he studies me with a worried frown. Several times he starts to say something, then stops. Most Norwegians speak perfect English, but it's different for some of the older generation.

Rain. At first one or two drops, then it hammers down. Olav grimaces and gestures below deck. I hurry down the steps after him, grateful when he makes his way to the far side of the ferry, furthest from the bar. I take off my coat and we sit next to each other in silence punctuated by awkward smiles.

To pass the time, I scroll through photos on my phone. Mormor's elkhound dog, Gandalf – I was so pleased when she let me name him; some shots of the harbour, and a selfie of us having a midnight picnic on the beach. In summer it never gets dark. They call it the land of the midnight sun, and that's how I think of it: a place where I was free and happy, an endless summer.

I come to a photo of Mormor at her spinning wheel, her long blonde hair in plaits. The evenings when she told stories were my favourite. My heart would thud to the beat of her foot as she spun her words into the yarn – filling the cabin with magic and wonder. Her tales usually revolved around my ancestors, women who had all kinds of strange adventures, but sometimes she would speak of the terrifying *draugr*, the dead who walk again at night or under the cover of fog. After one of her scarier stories I would insist on taking a candle to bed. 'Blow it out before you sleep now,' she'd say. 'You don't want the dead to find you!' I knew she was only joking, but some nights I lay awake in fear, every creak of the floorboards a walking corpse. When I called out, Mormor would be there, smoothing my hair and singing me a lullaby. Sometimes she would vow to stop telling me frightening stories, but they were my favourite ones and I would always ask to hear them again.

As we arrive at Skjebne, Olav grabs my rucksack and insists on carrying it. I thank him with one of the few words I know – '*Takk*' – and he rewards me with a thumbs up in reply. If only I knew the Norwegian to ask for a lift.

As I wait for the ferry doors to open, a grin spreads across my face. I made it! I actually made it! My smile doesn't last long. An icy gust slams into me, pushing me backwards. The wind screams past my ears as Olav's hand steadies me from behind.

No bullet can stop the dead.

I shudder and turn around, but there's only Olav. I'm sure I heard a raspy voice, but maybe it was just the wind.

I keep my head down and battle up the slope, boots crunching on ice as sharp as broken glass. Beneath me, waves suck and splash at the harbour wall. When I get to the top, what I see isn't Skjebne. At least not the Skjebne I know. The cheerful red fishermen's cabins that stand on stilts along the water's edge are gone. In their place are wooden huts the colour of dried blood, brooding over the waves with dark intent. Even the jagged mountains beyond seem sharper in their shroud of winter white.

I follow Olav as he trudges around the huts, the path beneath our feet obscured by mist. The red is faded in places. From a distance, it seemed as if they'd

21

been bleached by the sun, but looking up I see dozens of seagulls nesting under the dark pitched roofs. The vertical lines of white are streaks of birds' mess. In summer I loved to hear the gulls cry as they circled above the boat. It felt like my own special welcome party. With only the crash of waves and bluster of the wind, the night seems strangely quiet.

Olav walks past an old guesthouse with what looks like a 'for sale' sign, then enters a small gravel car park. Beyond it is a line of A-shaped wooden frames, taller than a house. In summer there would be hundreds of stockfish hanging down like fruit, drying in the sun. Now they're dark and empty, a gallows with no one to hang.

The throaty caw of a raven makes me jump. It swoops past my head, then lands on a wooden post. I step back, a little nervous. Most wild creatures don't get that close. But then I remember how Mormor used to feed a raven from her hand on the porch each morning . . . and these ones are probably just tame thanks to the tourists giving them titbits. The raven plumps its grey-feathered chest and fixes me with a beady stare before cawing again.

Olav gestures to an old blue Volvo, the only vehicle in the car park. I shout, '*Takk*,' but the wind whips away my words. He throws my bag onto the back seat and holds open the door, but I hesitate. Mum has warned me so many times never to get in a car with someone I don't know. But then Mormor has always seemed friendly with him and his wife, and it's got to be safer than walking in the dark on my own. I glance at the deserted car park and climb inside, happy to escape the sting of the wind.

Olav starts the engine and turns a dial to de-mist the windscreen. He sneaks a look at my eye, then coughs awkwardly. Even if he could speak English, I doubt he'd know what to say.

'*Bo hos mæ?*' He jabs a thumb to his chest. '*Hjemme til han Olav?*'

I shake my head, then rub my hands together. Even with my gloves, they are numb from the cold.

He tries again. 'Olav's *hus?*'

Finally I understand. Why does he want to take me to his place? Unease ripples through me. I reach for the door handle – maybe I should get out.

Olav looks alarmed. '*Med* Yrsa! Wife Yrsa!'

I smile with relief, but as much as I'm grateful for the lift, I haven't come all this way to see him or his wife.

'Mormor house. I want to see Mormor.'

Olav grips the wheel with both hands and gives me a serious look. Maybe he's worried about me travelling on my own. He starts to say something in Norwegian, but gives up when I shrug and smile apologetically.

He drives in silence, seemingly lost in thought. When he takes the road to Mormor's cabin, I sit a little taller. She'll be so surprised, I can't wait to see her. She'll throw an extra log on the stove and brew some coffee and I'll give her the cookies. After that I'll explain why I had to come.

Olav stops the car and I peer through the windscreen at Mormor's little cabin on top of the hill. Maybe it's the shadowy moonlight, but the plants on the roof look like they've doubled in size. Lots of rural buildings in Norway have living roofs as insulation, and Mormor is proud of the neat rows of herbs she grows in summer. Now the roof seems overgrown with weeds and there's even a miniature Christmas tree up there.

A light comes on. Good, she's still awake. Olav stares at the cabin, wide-eyed. Surely he isn't going to drop me here, at the end of a dirt track? He rubs a thumb across his lip and looks at the house and back to me. When I don't say anything, he drives up to the cabin and then points at the house. 'Mora di, yes?' I don't know what he means, but I nod anyway.

We get out of the car and he lifts my rucksack from the back seat. I grab it and we have an awkward tussle as he tries to carry it for me. In the end I hold it to myself with a firm *takk*. I know how Mormor likes to chat and I want her all to myself.

Olav offers me his bare hand, which I shake. Unable to say much else, I smile and repeat, '*Takk . . . takk . . .*' again and again. I honestly can't thank him enough. The idea of walking all that way in the dark makes me shudder. He raises his hand and says something else about *mora di*, then gets into his car and drives away.

Without the lights of the vehicle, the night is that much blacker. I turn to the cabin as a cloud drifts across the moon, throwing it into shadow. Like everything else, it looks different to when I've been in summer. Darker and smaller; hunched in on itself. I glance at the weeds rustling on the roof. They make the place seem neglected, abandoned almost.

A mound of logs sits next to the woodshed, waiting to be chopped. I walk past them, then climb the few rickety steps to the porch and knock at the wooden door. An icy drop of rain lands on my face, making me shiver. I wish I'd let Olav see me inside. I knock again, louder this time. Where is Mormor? Even if she was in the bath she should be able to hear. It's not exactly a big place.

A gust of wind flings grit in my face and I turn away. Then I catch sight of it. The twisted tree. At first it's just a blurred shape at the bottom of the garden, shaking in the breeze. I squint and its black branches come into focus. It looks even more gnarled and ancient than I remember. I don't blame the tree for the accident; it was my fault for losing my footing. Even so, seeing it makes me shiver.

Bang. Bang. Bang.

I hammer on the door and scan the windows. Suddenly the light inside goes out, plunging the porch into darkness. My heart leaps into my throat. Why would she turn it off? I blink as my sight adjusts to the pale moonlight. The wind is so loud Mormor can't have heard me knock, that's all. She must have turned off the light and gone to bed.

I peer through the dark window and see an oil lamp on the table, its flame dying. Mormor would never go to bed and leave a flame burning, even a low one. Something is wrong.

'Mormor, it's me, Martha!'

A shape inside the cabin darts past the window. My legs turn to water. I'm sure it was a man, bent low. Why is there a man in Mormor's kitchen? There has to be an explanation. Think, Martha. Where is Gandalf? Why isn't he barking? Maybe a burglar poisoned the dog. Or maybe Mormor went somewhere with him. Maybe she's looking after a sick neighbour, and that's what Olav was worrying about.

I grab my bag, the taste of vomit in my mouth. My hands shake as I scrabble for my phone. One bar. Even if I get through to Mum or Dad, what are they going to do?

My pulse quickens as a shadow races behind me. *Get a grip, would you?* It's just a cloud passing in front of the moon. But what if Mormor is in trouble and needs me? I can't stay out here. I sling my bag over my shoulder and gently nudge the door. It opens with a creak.

'Mormor?' My voice is barely a whisper. I reach to turn on the light, but I can't find the switch. I turn on the torch of my phone and hold it out before me, then lick my lips and swallow. The sound that comes from my mouth is a frightened squeak. 'I know there's someone in here. I saw you from outside.'

I scan the kitchen to my right. The oil lamp gutters on the wooden table, its flame casting strange shadows about the room. The little dresser is there with its row of blue flowery crockery. The colourful rag rug is where it should be. Mormor's books are all in place. The wooden chairs are tucked neatly under the table.

The kitchen smells strange – of boiled potatoes and vinegar. The tap drips with a rhythmic *plop*. A pan and dirty plates are stacked on the draining board. Mormor would never do that. What's going on?

My fingers tighten on the strap of my rucksack as I enter the open-plan living room. Embers glow red in the cast-iron stove to my left. It looks sinister in the dark: a pot-bellied monster on stumpy legs. Above it is the painting Mum did of the island, the choppy waves of the sea glinting in the half-light. The blue and white checked sofa facing it is empty. I go to the back of the cabin. Three more rooms: Mormor's bedroom, the spare room and the bathroom.

I walk on tiptoes, glancing in every direction. The creak of a floorboard makes me freeze. I spin to my left, expecting someone to jump out on my blind side, but there's just shadows. Forcing my legs to move, I make my way to Mormor's room. It's darker on this side of the cabin. I hold out my phone, but it only illuminates a tiny patch of wall. I hesitate outside her door.

Someone is breathing on the other side.

My heart skitters in my chest. I lean my ear against the wood and gasp. There's a faint shuffling sound.

What if they're doing something to Mormor? I have to stop them!

My hand trembles as I grasp the knob.

I open the door and scream. A boy is standing there. Tall and wiry, about the same age as me. He has long dark hair, a pale face and wears black eyeliner under his eyes. He stares at me and holds up his hands in a bizarre act of surrender, as if my phone is actually a gun.

Fear turns to rage. 'Who the hell are you?' For a crazy moment I think he must be an apparition, not a real human being. But a ghost wouldn't look so terrified.

'*Sorry!* I can explain, please. I can explain.' He says something in Norwegian, then tries again. 'Please, it's not what you think.'

My legs won't hold me a second longer. I collapse onto the bed while he stares at me like *I'm* the intruder.

'Where's my grandmother?'

He looks at me aghast, then says in a small voice, 'I only know what I heard.'

'Which is . . . ? What? Just tell me!'

'The woman who lived here is dead. Her funeral was last week.'

ROTTING LEAVES AND DEAD THINGS

'You're a tough cookie. You'll be OK.' That's what Dad said when he saw my eye. He might as well have patted me on the shoulder and said, 'I can't help you. You're on your own, kiddo.' Sitting on the bed, I pull the biscuits from my bag. I was going to share them with Mormor – my celebratory treat for making it here. For being a *tough cookie*.

She can't be dead, she just can't. Someone would have sent word to Mum; we would know! Or perhaps part of me did know, deep down. The thought is like a hand stirring murky waters, churning up mud and silt and allowing dark things to the surface. Tears stream down my face as I clench my hands into fists, crumbling the cookies to nothing. The world blurs to grey, everything gone but the ache in my chest.

Snot drips from my nose and I wipe it away with my sleeve. 'How did she . . . ?'

The boy glances behind me. 'In her sleep, I think.'

I turn and gaze at the bed. Mormor's colourful crocheted blanket looks painfully cheerful. Propped between two white pillows is the wonky heart-shaped cushion we made together when I was eight years old.

My grandmother died in the bed I'm sitting on.

I clasp my hand to my mouth. Mormor's things look so pitiful without her: a metal hairbrush with strands of blonde hair on the wooden dressing table, a string of pearls draped over the mirror above, a blue shawl hanging from the door of her huge oak wardrobe. On her bedside table, a photo of me and Mum in a silver frame, a glass of water and an embroidery in a wooden hoop with a pair of scissors. It's like she might walk back in at any minute.

I lean forward and yank open my rucksack. The boy jumps as I hurl my stuff at the floor. Pyjamas, jeans, trainers. My hands fly as if they don't belong to me. Why did I wait? I could have booked the plane ticket weeks ago. I should have been here!

The boy holds out a tissue. I snatch it and blow my nose while he hovers in the doorway like a forlorn dark angel. His face is so unusual – a straight nose, full lips and striking cat-shaped eyes. He wears the strangest things: a waistcoat over a black striped shirt, tight black jeans slashed on the thigh like a creature has clawed him, and black boots with metal spikes up the sides.

Anger twists inside me. 'You said you can explain. So explain.'

He casts his eyes to the floor and chooses his words carefully, as if afraid to get them wrong – though his English is perfect, with only a trace of a Norwegian accent. 'I'm sorry. I needed somewhere to sleep and the place was empty. I thought it would be OK.' He points to the door. 'I stayed in the other room. I didn't know someone would come.'

'You didn't know and you didn't care! Get out!'

I glance at the window as lightning flashes. The twisted tree jumps out of the night, its gnarled branches swaying wildly in the wind. For a horrible moment, I imagine it might come alive and march up to the cabin. Rain beats on the glass, a hundred tiny fists pounding to get in.

Looking at Mormor's things is more than I can bear. I turn back, but the boy has gone, like he was never there. As I step into the living room, a rush of icy air hits me. The boy is at the front door, silhouetted in moonlight. His black leather trench coat flaps about his ankles. Next to his feet is a bulging duffle bag, the sleeve of a white shirt hanging out the side. I presume his bag doesn't have Mormor's valuables inside, but how do I know?

He hoists it to his shoulder. 'I'm sorry.'

Ignoring him, I step into the kitchen and rest my back against the counter. Once I hear the door click

31

shut, I switch on the light and survey the dirty dishes. The boy didn't just help himself to Mormor's spare room, he raided her larder too. And he's been here for more than a couple of nights, unless he had his mates over. My fingernails dig into my palms. How dare he!

Exhausted, I slump into a chair and bury my face in my hands. Mormor should be sitting opposite me. We should be laughing and remembering good times. I wrote so many letters, asking her the same questions. Now all I have is an empty chair. Tears slide down my nose and plop onto the table. My head pounds with the injustice of it.

A moth flits around my head. I watch it in a daze, unable to move. Maybe the boy is wrong. Maybe he misunderstood and it was someone else's funeral. Maybe Mormor is visiting a friend. My shoulders sag. Mormor is dead. The truth of it is like a stone in my belly.

The moth's wings beat against the light bulb with a faint *tap, tap*. The light is so bright it feels wrong, like when Mum used to wake me at dawn for a school trip. I know life goes on, but perhaps this is how everything will be now: harsh and cold and wrong. The moth drops to the table with a tiny thud. Its thick body is covered with fur, its bug-eyed face part alien, part rat. Velvet-soft wings unfold to reveal two white unseeing eyes. Funny how things appear so different when you stop to look at them.

I don't know how long I sit with my head on the table – until my legs are numb from the cold and my arm throbs with pins and needles. Sitting here won't bring her back. With a heavy sigh I go to the front door and slide the bolt shut.

I make my way to the spare bedroom, the one I shared with Mum whenever we visited. On each side of the room is a single bed built into its own little nook. The carved wooden frames are painted grey-blue and stencilled with yellow and red flowers. With blue velvet drapes to close out the night chill, it was like sleeping in a fairy tale. One of the beds is messed up now, sheets tangled with crocheted covers, and the room smells faintly of boy. I close the door and go to Mormor's room, where I crawl into bed with a sob.

I'm running through fog, but no matter how fast I run, I can't escape the twisted tree. Its gnarled arms snatch at my hair and tear at my clothes as thick roots erupt from the earth and grab my ankles. Mormor has her back to me and is grasping for a piece of cloth hanging from a branch, even though it's hopelessly out of her reach. I cry out and she turns to face me, and her eyes are two black orbs.

And then I'm inside the hollow chamber of the tree, knee deep in rotting leaves and dead things. Dirty black claws reach for me and I scream in terror. I'm sinking fast, up to my waist, my chest. Falling into the earth itself.

'Mormor,' I sob. 'Please, I need you. Please, you can't be gone . . . Mormor!'

I shudder with relief, my mind somewhere between sleep and waking. It's OK, it's just a dream . . . And then the real nightmare slams into my head: Mormor is dead.

My eyes snap open to darkness and for a second I'm back in hospital, my eyes bandaged tight. My heart hammers in my chest. Why can't I see? And then the shape of the huge wardrobe looms into view. I'm not blind – it's just dark. I take a deep breath and try to stop my panic.

They kept my eyes bandaged for nine days. It was horrible, but nothing compared to the terror of being told I might not see again. I was never really scared of the dark before. At home there's a street lamp outside my bedroom window that offers a constant reassuring glow. After the accident I would pull back one of the curtains before I got into bed. That way I never had to open my eyes to blackness.

Lying here now, the darkness has a weight. It presses against my skin as I reach for the covers and curl into a ball. I long for the oblivion of sleep but my mind won't let me. My thoughts probe the rawness inside me like a tongue touching a sore spot in a mouth.

Something woke me just now – a noise. I glance at unfamiliar shadows and strain to hear beyond the desolate wail of the storm. Nothing. Perhaps I dreamed it.

A dog barks. A sharp noise, high above the howl of the wind.

Someone must be looking after Gandalf. He wouldn't have been left to fend for himself, surely? I remember all the summers we spent together. I used to love curling up with him by the fire, my fingers in his soft fur. He would push his head against me until I rubbed him behind his ears, and in return he'd lick my nose.

I prop myself up on one elbow and listen as the wind builds to a troubled moan. Maybe Gandalf nudged his way into the woodshed and the wind banged the door shut. He might be trapped inside. Poor thing, it must be freezing out there.

Another bark.

Mormor keeps a torch on the kitchen dresser. I could put on my coat and take a look. I shiver and pull the blanket tighter. The shed isn't far, but the thought of leaving the cabin scares me.

More barking, louder this time.

I can't leave him out there.

I stand and feel for the light switch, my fingers exposed in the darkness as they roam the cold wall. The light comes on and my shoulders drop with relief. The electricity has always been temperamental, especially in bad weather; that's why Mormor kept oil lamps. Not that we needed them much in summer, as it never really got dark. A horrible thought crawls into my mind. It's late winter now – that means there will only be a few hours of light.

In the kitchen, I shrug into my coat and boots. My breath hangs on the air as I reach for the torch on the

35

dresser. The heavy metal casing is freezing but feels reassuringly solid in my hand. I click the button and it flickers into life: not exactly bright but better than getting my phone wet.

I open the cabin door and the icy rain is like a thousand needles stinging my face. The cold is so shocking I have to remind myself to breathe. Inhaling the salt smell of the sea, I step into the night. It's two miles from here to the coast, but now there are no fields dotted with yellow flowers, and no twinkling sea beyond – just a slab of black. The island's vast spaces – its long sweeping beaches, jagged mountains and dense forests – didn't worry me in summer, but in the dark . . . I don't like to think what might be out there.

Making my way down the rickety steps, I sweep the torch across the path and see weed stalks dripping with water. I long to shine the beam into the darkness but I know the light will be swallowed up; better to keep it pointed down.

Clouds drift apart to reveal a glimpse of moonlight, sending shadows racing over the ground. My body tenses. Someone is watching me. I shake the idea from my head but the thought creeps up and taps me on the shoulder, insistent.

The beam shakes as I point the torch at the wooden shed. Swallowing my fear, I force my feet to move. There's something to my left. A shadow at the edge of my vision. I turn, heart pounding.

Just wind and rain.

It's because you can't see from that side, I tell myself. *Nothing is going to jump out at you.*

A raven's caw cuts through the night. I startle and the torch thuds to the ground. 'Shit!' I grab it and stab uselessly at the button. Before me, the shed door bangs lightly in the wind. It hasn't been latched on the outside – it must have got caught on something inside. My palms burn despite the cold. I start to nudge the door when I hear scratching.

My voice is tiny. 'Gandalf? Is that you?'

I push the door and something leaps out at me. I gasp and stumble backwards. 'Gandalf!'

He throws himself against my legs and I kneel to accept his frenzied licks. He's much bigger than I remember. His head and body are heavyset, his thick silver fur warm despite the cold.

'You poor thing! How long have you been here?'

I run my hand along his back and curly tail. 'Good boy! It's good to see you too!' He licks my face and I hug him, breathing in his familiar smell. His warmth is so comforting I don't want to let him go. I hadn't realised how much I missed him until now.

A shadow shifts inside the shed. The dog moves towards it.

'Gandalf, stay!'

He weaves around a pile of wood before I can stop him. I desperately jab at the torch and it flickers into life. Directing the beam reveals a stack of logs, an old axe and a dark shape on the ground. A white face with long black hair blinks at me.

'You!'

He sits up and holds an arm to his eyes. 'I'm sorry. I had nowhere to go.'

A green sleeping bag covers his legs, and he's been using his duffel bag as a pillow.

'Why didn't you tell me about Gandalf?'

'Who?'

'Mormor's dog. Why didn't you tell me he was here?'

Gandalf covers the boy's face in a barrage of licks and he smiles and scratches the dog's head in return. 'I only met him tonight. I heard barking so I let him in with me.'

Gandalf puts his head on one side, his brown eyes pleading. It must be well below zero – the boy will freeze if he stays out here. He left the cabin when I told him to, but even so, I know nothing about him. I can't just let him back in.

Gandalf barks as if determined to change my mind. I bite my lip, wishing Mormor was here. What would she do? In her stories, a stranger always turns out to be a powerful wizard. Those who offer meat and mead are rewarded but those who close their doors pay the price. It wasn't in Mormor's nature to turn anyone away. I look up to see Gandalf licking the boy's nose. He would know if the boy was bad, surely.

I turn towards the door. 'Come on, let's get you inside.'

Gandalf wags his tail and trots towards me, then stops and glances back. The boy is wearing his leather coat inside the sleeping bag. I walk over to him with a sigh, hating the idea of touching his clothes, but at the same time knowing it's the only way to tell if I can trust him.

Standing above him, I take a deep breath and steel myself for whatever comes. I reach my fingers to the back of his shoulder, in a gesture that hopefully looks like I want him to get up. Thoughts and feelings crowd my mind. Guilt, love and sadness – then another emotion: one of bitterness, jealousy and hatred. How can someone carry so much kindness and yet have the potential for such malice too? It's like he has a split personality. I pause, unsure. There is nothing to suggest he wants to hurt me, but something isn't right.

The boy looks at me hopefully, his teeth chattering. Gandalf barks and I shrug reluctantly. 'Come on then, get up, before you freeze to death.'

He hastily grabs his stuff and follows me up the porch steps and into the cabin. I close the door behind us, then kneel down and scratch the dog between the ears. Holding his head between my hands, I stare into his eyes. What am I doing, Gandalf? I don't know this guy and he broke into my grandmother's house. My *dead* grandmother's house.

Gandalf grins – he has one of those doggy faces that's always smiling – and wags his tail so hard it might drop off. I watch in wonder as he sits at the boy's feet and stares up at him. The boy pats the dog with a smile, and anger rises inside me. 'It's just for tonight.'

'Thank you. I won't get in your way.' He holds out his hand. 'My name is Stig.'

'Martha.'

Perhaps realising I'm in no mood for formal greetings, he clasps his hands behind his back and smiles awkwardly, revealing two perfect dimples. The way he rocks on his heels, he could be a gentleman from another era, not a twenty-first-century goth boy.

My coat pocket vibrates. I must have forgotten to switch off the alarm. I blink at the screen in surprise: 8.00 a.m. But Norway is an hour on; that means it's nine o'clock here. How can it be morning when it's pitch black outside?

Stig seems to read my mind. 'Won't get light for an hour or so.'

I glance at the dark kitchen window. No point trying to sleep now. I may as well clean up. I put some food and water down for Gandalf, then start on the dishes, ignoring Stig's insistent offers to help. When I'm done, I grab a chair to my left, but misjudge the distance and slump down awkwardly, nearly falling over.

Stig reaches out a hand. 'Are you O—'

I glare at him, my face hot with embarrassment.

He holds up his hands and takes a quick step back. 'Sorry, sorry!'

The way he says it reminds me of the boys on the ferry. I rest my chin in my hands, wondering if things could get any worse.

Stig loiters at the edge of my vision. 'Can I get you some coffee maybe?'

My head throbs as if I haven't slept for days. I give the briefest nod, then rub my temples. The sound of the water boiling in the saucepan is weirdly mundane. I guess there's no need to tell him where to find things. I watch him slide out a drawer and pick out a teaspoon. He looks totally at home. It only annoys me more. He spoons coffee grounds into the saucepan, but doesn't crack an egg into the mixture first, like Mormor used to. After a few minutes' boiling in the pan, he pours the coffee through a metal sieve balanced over a clay pot.

He hands me one of Mormor's flowery blue china cups, the ones she keeps for special occasions. I try not to let it bother me, but it does. Stig points at the chair opposite and I gesture for him to sit.

'So how come you have nowhere to go?' I ask.

Stig shifts in his seat. 'My stepfather. Everyone must see things his way. I didn't.'

'Do you live on the island?'

He shakes his head. 'Oslo.'

'That's miles away. How did you end up here?'

'I came to Skjebne for a holiday with my dad once.' A shadow of sadness crosses his face. He pulls his coat around him, then shrugs and adds, 'It seemed a nice place.'

I sip my coffee. It doesn't taste like Mormor's. I used to think it was funny how she mixed the coffee grounds with egg, but she was right. It does make it taste less bitter.

Stig raises an eyebrow. 'No good?'

'No egg,' I mutter, then bite my thumbnail. A habit from childhood I should have outgrown, according to my mum. 'So you didn't know anyone, or have anywhere to stay?'

'I had six thousand Kroner, enough to stay at the hotel on the harbour, but someone stole my wallet while I was asleep on the ferry. I didn't realise until I got off.'

His eyes are the palest blue, made even more startling by the black eyeliner. He holds my gaze, his face seemingly earnest, but what do I know? Maybe he *was* robbed, or maybe he came here to rob Mormor.

'So what made you choose this place to break into?'

Stig lowers his eyes to the table. 'I heard some women at the harbour talking about a lady who lived alone by the forest. They said she had died in her sleep, and had left a note saying she wanted her cabin kept stocked with food, ready for her daughter to visit. The other said the daughter knew about the funeral but wasn't coming.'

The blood drains from my head, making me feel sick. Mum knew Mormor had died! She knew about the funeral! Stig carries on talking but my mind is spinning so much I barely hear him. When was Mum planning to tell me exactly? Burning Mormor's letters is one thing, but how could she betray me like that?

Stig mumbles into his coffee. 'I walked up to the forest and found the cabin.'

My fists clench. 'So you just broke in?'

He swallows and licks his lips. 'The door was open. I only meant to stay for one night, but when no one came . . .'

'You made yourself at home.'

He lowers his head. 'I'm sorry.'

I can't believe how people can be so selfish. I open my mouth to tell him what I think of him, when Gandalf barks at the door. The yellow headlights of a car sweep into the room and Stig jumps up and grabs his bag. He stares at me accusingly, his body tense, alert.

I shrug like it's no big deal, but inside I'm jumping with nerves. I'm not exactly expecting company either, and the last thing I want is for Mum to know I'm here.

THERE'S SOMETHING OUT THERE

Stig glares at the door, then back to me. Anyone would think the police were after him. Anxiety coils in my stomach . . . When I touched his coat there was so much jealousy and anger. Maybe he's hurt someone and he's on the run.

I peek through the yellow checked curtains to see Olav's Volvo parked outside. 'It's OK, it's just a neighbour,' I whisper.

A knock sounds at the door and Stig's face turns white. His eyeliner is smudged and there are wood chips in his hair. Not that I'm much better. I haven't washed or brushed my hair since yesterday morning. With my ugly eye, I must look a fright.

A woman's red face peers through a gap in the

curtains, making us both startle. 'Marta? It is Yrsa!' A shower of taps assaults the window. Stig hurries to the back of the living room, and for a moment I wonder if he's going to crouch behind Mormor's flowery sofa.

'What will you tell her?' he hisses.

'Don't worry, it'll be OK,' I mutter.

More pounding, loud enough to wake the dead. The door shakes as someone tries it from outside. I rush and slide back the bolt. A tired and tense-looking Olav and a huge woman in a sheepskin coat stand on the porch. Yrsa, I presume. Several inches taller and a foot wider than Olav, she makes a formidable figure. Her cheeks are covered with a mass of red thread veins; it looks as if she's been butchering meat and hasn't stopped to wipe her face. What's so urgent they had to come this early?

Yrsa's brown eyes glitter as she raises a gloved hand to her eye and looks down at mine. Her voice is a deep rumble. 'The tree do that?'

I swallow and give a tiny nod.

Yrsa frowns at me as if I'm far too old to be climbing trees. 'How?'

I shrug and look away. The doctor said it's not uncommon for the mind to delete the moments before a major injury occurs and my memories will come back when they're ready, but I hate not being able to remember. I haven't climbed the tree since I was kid . . . the truth is I don't even know what I was doing up there.

Yrsa huffs and glances behind me. '*Mora di?*' I shake my head and she tries again. '*Mora di* – your mother? She is with you, yes?'

Mora di, that's what Olav kept saying when he dropped me off last night. Of course, when he saw the light on he was asking about Mum, presuming she was in the cabin. He was hardly going to guess Goldilocks the Goth had taken up residence.

'No, Mum isn't here.' I keep the door half closed. Even from here I can sense Stig's panic. If there was a back door, I'm sure he would have bolted by now.

Yrsa mutters something in Norwegian and Olav shrinks back. She pulls herself up to her full impressive height. 'We come in.' It's not a request.

I stand to one side, but not fast enough. As Yrsa pushes past me, a feeling of great strength and pride spreads through my chest. Sheepskin doesn't offer many impressions – it's like a musical instrument that only plays one note, but that note is loud and true. It speaks of a person's core essence, and Yrsa resonates warrior with every fibre of her being.

Gandalf bounds over with an excited bark and Olav drops to one knee. I don't know who gives the other more kisses. Yrsa pats the dog's head affectionately. 'You make us worried! Of course you come here, naughty runaway!'

The door of the bathroom gives a tiny squeak and Yrsa straightens. 'Who is there?' She takes a step forward and Stig cautiously enters the room.

Yrsa's eyebrows jump in surprise. 'Who are you?' She

looks him up and down, taking in his strange clothes and woodland hair accessories.

I speak without thinking. 'A friend of the family,' then stare at the floor, annoyed with myself for not just telling her the truth.

Gandalf trots around the sofa and sits obediently at Stig's feet. Boy and dog plead at me with their eyes and I give a tiny shake of my head. I feel bad that Stig ended up sleeping in the woodshed, but even so, I don't like lying for him.

Stig steps forward and holds out his hand. '*Jeg heter Stig.*' He approaches Yrsa confidently, like he's meant to be here. She asks him several questions in Norwegian and nods as he answers. Seemingly satisfied, she strides into the kitchen and takes off her scarf and gloves and puts them on the table, then opens a cupboard. She mutters and opens another. Stig raises an eyebrow and I shrug in reply. I've no idea what she's doing, and I'm not about to ask.

A cupboard door bangs shut, revealing Yrsa's fearsome face. 'How old is Stig?'

Stig starts to answer but Yrsa raises a hand to silence him. I glance at him and swallow, trying to guess his age. 'Erm, seventeen.'

Stig nods and I sigh with relief, but Yrsa isn't finished. 'And when Stig arrive?'

My words come out slow, unsure. 'He came a few days ago. He was hoping to go to the funeral, but he got the timing wrong.' I must have said the right thing as Stig relaxes slightly.

Yrsa nods, then starts a new line of questioning. 'Why your mother not here?'

I clench my jaw. 'Mum was meant to come but there was an emergency at work. She's going to fly out soon.' The truth burns like acid in my stomach. Mum robbed me of the chance to say goodbye to the person I loved most in the world.

Yrsa studies me. 'When she come?'

'Tomorrow, I think. It depends on flights.'

Yrsa nods but her face is blank; I've no idea whether she believes me. She catches Olav's attention, then says to me, 'We have family visiting. They go soon but no place for you tonight. If your mother come tomorrow, is OK you stay here?'

I nod and she pulls out a chair and gestures for me to sit. I lower myself cautiously, fearful of what she might say. Leaning on the table, she looks into my right eye and delivers her words slowly, each one a gift. 'Your *mormor*, she wanted cupboards kept full for you. She love you very much. She knew you would come, even if your mother did not.'

Tears sting my eyes at the mention of Mormor's name. 'At the end, was she . . . ?' I swallow and try again. 'Did she suffer? Was she ill, or . . . ?'

Yrsa hesitates a moment and then shakes her head. 'She died in her sleep. I found her full at peace.' Her voice is steady but there is uncertainty in her eyes. She glances at Olav and I wait for her to say more, but she doesn't.

'*Nei, du lyver!*' exclaims Stig.

48

I look over to see him talking to Olav. Judging by the surprised look on Stig's face, I'm guessing it's not good news. Yrsa says something to them both, her voice tense. She gives me a sideways look, then turns back and carries on talking in Norwegian.

Why do I have the feeling that she's keeping something from me? Maybe Mormor didn't die in peace. Maybe something terrible happened but she doesn't want to tell me. When she's not looking, I reach for her scarf. As soon as I touch it, uneasiness crowds my mind. The wool speaks of her affection for Mormor, but there's something else there too – a vague and nameless fear.

Yrsa snatches the scarf and the connection is lost. She fixes me with a look that's part accusatory, part wary, and I have an uncomfortable feeling of being caught out, as if she knows what I was doing. The unease she felt about Mormor she has for me too. I watch as she puts on her gloves and scarf, wanting to ask her about it, but not knowing how.

Stig's voice breaks the silence. 'Martha?'

He looks at me as if he's waiting, and I realise I can't have heard him before.

'Sorry, what?'

'Olav says we need to stay inside the cabin, at least for a few days. He's worried there's something out there.'

I glance at the dark window. 'What do you mean, out there?'

Stig exchanges a few hurried words with Olav and

the old man strokes his beard. '*Gaupe? Ulv?*' Stig turns back to me. 'A lynx maybe, or a wolf, he's not sure.'

Yrsa grunts. 'Sheep have been killed this past week. Their guts . . .' She draws a hand over her middle and pulls a face. 'Olav went to mainland for gun.'

A shiver runs through me. So that's what was in the metal case. I think back to what I heard when I got off the ferry – *No bullet can stop the dead* – but it doesn't make sense. The voice I heard wasn't Olav's; it didn't even sound human.

Yrsa stands with her hands on her hips. 'You have oil for lamps, yes?'

I look at her, my mind blank.

She squats and opens the cupboard under the sink. 'Yes, enough oil, I think.' She pats her legs and stands with a grunt. Her huge form takes up half the kitchen; she looks like she could wrestle a wolf herself.

'The dark can make people's minds . . .' Yrsa frowns as if she can't find the words, then starts again. 'The dark, it can play tricks – up here.' She taps a hand against her temple and I expect her face to soften, but it doesn't.

Olav opens the door but Yrsa hesitates. She touches her scarf and for a moment I think she is going to say something about it, but she just clears her throat, and I convince myself that I imagined the knowing look she gave me.

'Your *mormor*, she asked me strange thing. She wanted me to water the tree from the well if your mother or you no come. It has rained lately, so I haven't

50

watered it.' A look of regret crosses Yrsa's face but she shakes her head and it goes as quickly as it came. Her voice is brisk. 'Your mother come tomorrow. Don't go far from house, and you'll be OK.' She looks Stig up and down, then pats the dog's head. 'Gandalf can stay with you. He will keep you safe.'

Once they have driven away, silence descends on the cabin. Stig gives me a furtive glance and I wonder if he feels it too. The vast emptiness of outside crowding in – almost like it's a living, breathing thing in the room with us. Yrsa and Olav live miles away on the other side of the forest. Apart from them, there's no one. No phone or Internet connection, no way to contact the outside world. I was cut off in my room back in England, but at least I had Kelly and Mum for company. Apart from Gandalf, all I have now is a stranger.

Dead Men Rise with the Mist

I make some toast and coffee and Stig holds out his hands. Instinctively I flinch away in case his clothes touch me, then place the plate and cup on the kitchen table – managing to misjudge the distance and spilling coffee on his lap. He smiles forgivingly and I sit across from him, my face burning. I take a bite and chew quietly, feeling awkward.

Finally he breaks the silence. 'So your mother, she's coming out tomorrow?'

'I only told Yrsa that. Mum has no intention of coming.' I don't even try to hide the bitterness in my voice. He looks at me for an explanation, but how can I explain when I don't understand myself. Mum never exactly got on with Mormor, but after the accident her moods became so erratic. One minute she'd be worried and fussing over me, the next she'd be cross with me for even mentioning Mormor's name.

'It's tricky.' I shrug. 'What about you? Can you get your mum to send you some money for the ferry?'

Stig gives a hollow laugh. 'No. I'd rather sleep in the woodshed than go back.'

I bite my thumbnail, knowing how that feels. 'It's complicated,' says Stig. Then under his breath, 'Complicated like a labyrinth.'

I think about all the hours I've spent reading Mum's clothing, testing the different types of material and trying to understand her. Once when she went out, I even climbed the loft ladder and went through an old chest of her clothes. I know she loves me, but there's so much she keeps hidden.

'Try a labyrinth in the dark,' I sigh.

'Blindfolded,' says Stig.

'With a big hairy Minotaur,' I add.

'So, you've met my mother?' Stig gives a wry smile and I start to laugh, then stop. It feels wrong without Mormor here to share the joke.

'What about you? Are you going to go home?' asks Stig.

I glance at the door. 'I'd rather sleep in the shed with you.' He raises an eyebrow and I feel myself blushing. 'Not *with* you. I meant . . .'

'I know, don't worry.' He inspects his nail, then says in a quiet voice, 'Maybe we can both stay here for a while?'

I shift in my seat. 'I guess. For a few days anyway.'

He looks relieved, but my chest is tight with anxiety. I can't throw him out with nowhere to go, especially now I've lied to Yrsa, but I'm not exactly comfortable with him being here. Better to let him think he can only stay for a couple of nights.

I sigh, feeling trapped inside. My body feels heavy, like when I've taken out the bathplug but stayed in the water. For months the cabin is the only place I've wanted to be, but now Mormor has gone, I don't know what to do. I can't face going home and seeing Mum. Right now I never want to see her again.

Stig looks in the wicker basket and throws the last remaining log on the fire. 'Is there some way I can help? Anything at all? I could take you to the graveyard in the village perhaps?' There is kindness in his eyes, as if he really cares. I give a half-smile, touched by his concern. A part of me would like to see where Mormor is buried, but I don't know if I'm ready. If I stay here, surrounded by her things, then it's like she hasn't really gone. Going to her grave would mean having to say goodbye. I shake my head.

'Well, just say if you change your mind.'

I look out of the window, feeling uncomfortable under Stig's scrutiny. 'Anyway, aren't we meant to stay inside in case there's a wolf or something?'

Stig snorts. 'It will just be a stray dog. I'm sure Olav will shoot it soon.'

I pull my heavy woollen cardigan a little tighter, then glance around the cabin. Stig's gaze meets mine and we smile at each other shyly. Although he's a complete stranger, there's something about him that seems vaguely familiar. 'A spark of connection', is what Kelly calls it, when you meet someone and feel like you know them already.

My phone buzzes. Then buzzes again. And again.

'Reception comes and goes,' explains Stig. 'You get nothing, then everything at once.'

Several texts from Mum and one from Kelly: *How's it going hun? Missed you last night x*. I clasp the charm around my neck and start to type: *Mormor is d—*, then delete it. I can't bring myself to say it. Instead I send: *Busy but talk soon. Luv u x*

I watch Stig leave the cabin, then look back at my phone. Mum will be expecting me to text – if I don't contact her, she might phone Dad. At least she won't call his house, not when there's a chance Chantelle might answer. Chantelle was Dad's secretary before he gave her the job of mistress and then promoted her to wife. She's fifteen years younger than Mum, has fake boobs, fake eyelashes and a fake tan. To make it worse, she's totally genuine in every other way and couldn't be lovelier if she tried. It doesn't bother me he's got someone new – Dad checked out of our lives years ago; I just wish Mum could move on.

In the end I message: *Am fine, having a good time at Dad's.* I don't put a kiss.

According to my phone it's 10.45 a.m., yet it's only just properly light. I look out the window to see the sky swollen with rain clouds. Stig emerges from the woodshed clutching an axe. He props it next to the porch, then takes off his coat and rolls up his sleeves. I watch his body twist and turn as he chops, the rhythmic swing of his arm hypnotising. The blade hits the wood with a satisfying thump and scrape. He throws the split logs aside and reaches for another. With his spiked boots and slashed jeans he should look out of place, yet he doesn't. He looks at ease, like this is his home.

Stig glances at the window and I duck away. A few minutes later I watch as he strips off his waistcoat and rolls up his shirtsleeves. His body is lean and wiry with well-defined arms, as if he's used to physical work. Kelly would say he's hot, but then she says that about every boy she meets.

The pile of wood is dwindling. Soon there will be nothing left to split and he'll come back indoors. Anxiety flutters inside me. I know so little about him, yet we're going to be living together, at least for a while. Seeing him wield a weapon like a professional axe murderer isn't exactly reassuring.

I drop the curtain and turn to the room. The cabin feels so empty without Mormor. Memories cluster like spiderwebs in every corner: the shells we collected from the beach; the rag rug we made together; the feathers we found on a walk.

Pocketing my phone, something occurs to me. Even if Mum burned her letters, Mormor would have received the ones I sent. I wrote half a dozen times. She would have known about my ability to read clothes and how desperate I've been to understand it. If Mormor asked Yrsa to keep the cupboards stocked, maybe she left a message for me. I jump to my feet with excitement. Yrsa said she'd known I would come.

Hoping to find an envelope with my name on it, I go to the shelf of photographs above the stove and lift a frame. My face from two years ago beams out at me. I recognise the long blonde hair, skinny arms and freckles, but it's like looking at a stranger – and not just because of the matching pair of eyes. In the picture I'm wearing a white bikini and shading my face from the sun: a tanned and happy fifteen-year-old on holiday, without a care in the world. I check behind the frame – no hidden letter – then put the past back where it belongs.

Next to my picture is a photo of Mormor, laughing at something off-camera. She looks flushed, as if she's been dancing. Her long blonde hair hangs in plaits and she's wearing her bunad, a traditional Norwegian costume, embroidered with flowers. I lift the frame and run my finger across her face. You can tell from her cheekbones that she must have been stunning in her youth. Even in her seventies she radiated beauty and warmth.

As I put the picture back, three old photos drop out. Black and white, each one shows a different woman, all with long blonde hair. One is posed stiffly at a spinning wheel, scowling. Her wavy hair is parted in the centre, there are dark circles under her eyes and her childlike mouth is pursed. Despite the scowl, you can see the family resemblance to Mormor. Another shows a tiny old woman wearing a cloak of dark feathers. She sits in the branches of a tree, her eyes as black and shiny as a bird's. In the third, a woman hunches over a steaming cauldron, bundles of wool on the ground.

I'm sure I've seen these women before, and then I realise. The photos show the women from Mormor's tales: my great-grandmother Karina who muttered spells at the spinning wheel, Gerd who stitched a cloak of feathers so that she could fly, and vain Trine with her cauldron of dyed wool. But they were just fairy tales. They can't be true.

Mormor would never tell me what the women in my family had really been like. When I asked, she would laugh and say I already knew their stories. Once I asked her about her life as a child. I could sense her excitement as she described how her mother, my great-grandmother Karina, had taught her to stitch as soon as she was old enough to hold a needle. Mormor handed me a half-done embroidery and several lengths of thread, but then Mum came in and the air turned to ice.

I examine the painting above the stove. There are so many shades of light and dark in the sky, Mum has captured the bay perfectly. She hasn't painted anything for so long, I'd forgotten how talented she is.

Looking at the painting makes me think about all the summers we've spent playing and walking on the beach here. The last few holidays started off sunny, but within days I would sense an argument brewing between Mum and Mormor, hanging over us like an impending storm. After Mum and Dad got divorced, Mormor wanted Mum and me to move to Skjebne permanently. She asked so many times, and it always ended in a row.

I know Mormor and Mum kept secrets from me. They passed them back and forth to one another, like a stitch made over and over, until they became fastened into the fabric of our lives. I turn my back to the painting and sigh, annoyed at myself for not making them tell me. But I loved coming to the island, and the more questions I asked, the angrier Mum got. It became easier not to ask.

Mormor's cashmere shawl is folded on the side of the armchair. Perhaps it's not too late to unpick the truth.

I step towards it and reach out my hand. Taking a deep breath, I clear my mind, ready for whatever emotions come. My fingers graze the soft material and my heart races. Despair, guilt, fear. Mormor grabbing Yrsa's hand, begging and pleading.

I cry out and pull away. Yrsa lied to me! Mormor didn't die peacefully. She died in anguish.

I rush to the door and snatch it open, desperate for air.

'Hey, look at this!' Stig points towards the sea, but he doesn't have to – I see it: a massive wall of fog as high as a cliff. I watch, unable to believe my eyes, as streams of mist cascade down like a waterfall.

When the fog rises, run for home, Marta, my child. Dead men rise with the mist!

I shiver at the memory of Mormor's words. I know her stories were harmless – a way to ensure a little girl who liked to roam didn't get lost in the fog, but I was always afraid, as if she could make the impossible happen just by saying it.

I close my eyes, wishing I had never touched her shawl. What could have made her so upset? Maybe she was begging Yrsa to get Mum, only she wouldn't come.

I grab my coat and go out. The fog must be at least a mile away, but I can feel its clammy chill on my face. The axe drops from Stig's hand and lands with a dull thump. 'Å *faen* . . . It's getting closer!'

We stand side by side and watch the tsunami of cloud move insidiously towards us. We could be the only two people left on Earth, waiting for the apocalypse to come. 'Stig, maybe we should get inside.' I scan the horizon. 'Where's Gandalf?'

Stig picks up his clothes and shrugs back into them. 'He was here just now, sniffing that old tree.'

While Stig watches the fog, I walk around the cabin to the garden. Not that you can call it a garden – more a few acres of grass less tall than the surrounding heath. I often saw Mormor scrubbing dirt from her nails at the kitchen sink, yet there are no flower beds or vegetable patches. Once when I woke early, she was on her knees weeding around the roots of the twisted tree.

I pause before it now, my heart pounding. It stands on its own grassy mound, like it was planted there deliberately. Three times the height of the cabin, its enormous grey trunk is a mass of bulges and knots, and so big it would take seven of me with arms outstretched to encircle it. Thick green moss coats the base of its trunk: a plush velvet skirt covering the rough, scaly bark. The wind has died to nothing and for once its mighty branches barely stir.

It looks so different to when I came in summer. Menacing almost. Keeping my distance, I walk around it, stepping over knobbly roots that protrude from the earth like the veins on a hand. One of the huge roots contains a deep pool of water. Mormor said it holds a natural spring, and that's why it never dries up.

Where *is* that dog? 'Gandalf!' I scan the dark edge of the forest. The fir trees crowd together like soldiers in battle formation, their trunks forming a hard drawn line. We should have kept Gandalf on a long rope. What if he's wandered off and there really is a wolf?

I trudge through orange spiky bracken, shouting now.

'Hey, wait!' Stig yells behind me.

I turn to see a looming mountain of fog. It smothers the light, giving the world an eerie feel. Water glistens in Stig's hair, like dew on a spiderweb.

'Gandalf – where exactly did you see him last?' I call, my voice breathless.

Stig points. 'He was digging there, by the tree.'

I clamber back over the bracken. 'And you didn't call him back?'

Stig's eyes are wide with worry.

'Gandalf!' we shout together.

'Is that him?' I point at the twisted tree. 'There! I thought I saw something move.'

We jog to the tree then stop, both at the same time, as if we've hit an invisible wall.

Inside its huge gnarled trunk are several hollow chambers, formed by the weird way the tree has grown. As a child I used to love playing in the dark spaces, but I would often have bad dreams about them too. Sometimes I think the tree has always been on the edge of my nightmares, waiting to trip my feet and snatch at my hair.

When I was younger I could easily stand up in the largest chamber, but now I have to bend almost double. I peer inside and the back of my neck prickles. There's a black hole three times the size of a rabbit hole, the wood around it scored as if someone has cut it with a knife. I blink against the gloom, unable to believe what I'm seeing. Blackness emanates from it, growing bigger and then smaller. A dark, pulsating heart.

Buzzing fills the air, like a swarm of flies or the rush of water but higher pitched – the sound of an electrical current almost. A stench of decay sends a wave of revulsion through my stomach. It feels like we've stumbled across a decomposing body covered in rotten leaves. We shouldn't be here. I want to move, but I can't.

A loud bark breaks the spell. Gandalf is on the porch, growling ferociously as if we are the ones who need saving. He jumps in circles, barking madly. Warning us to run.

A Howl Shatters the Night

I slam the door and drag the bolt across. Stig is doubled over, palms on his knees, panting hard. Droplets of water cling to his hair and clothes 'You OK?' he asks. I shake my head, unable to speak. 'You're fast! I couldn't keep up,' he laughs.

My lips twitch upward but I don't feel like smiling. There's something wrong with that tree. Unnatural. I inhale deeply through my nose but my stomach won't stop churning. Just the memory of that putrid smell makes me want to heave. The hole can't have been there when I came last summer, I would have noticed. It seemed too big to have been dug by an animal, yet the grooves in the wood looked like claw marks.

Stig peers out the window. 'The fog is right on top of us!' He wipes his breath from the glass and gestures for me to look. The world outside is gone, replaced by a dense uniform grey. Mist swirls over the porch, wrapping itself around the balustrades like a scarf looking for a neck to strangle. The room darkens as fog drifts across the window, devouring us whole. The cabin is freezing, colder than I've ever known. I look at the stove, expecting to see a pile of ash, but the embers glow orange.

'Did you notice anything funny – I mean, odd? Just now, outside?'

Stig shushes the dog, who growls at the door as if Death itself were standing on the porch. 'You mean Gandalf? Dogs can be affected by the weather. He'll be fine.'

I sit on the sofa and shiver as a ribbon of mist wisps in through the keyhole. I was sure Stig had felt it too – he must have noticed the awful smell and strange noise, but he wanders from the room, humming under his breath. Maybe it's all in my head. Mum says I have a vivid imagination, just like Mormor.

Gandalf snaps at his tail. I don't know whether he's afraid, excited or preparing to fight – and I don't think he knows either.

Stig reappears holding a towel. 'Do you want to wash first? There might not be much hot water. It can take a while to heat up.' He grins good-naturedly, but I don't smile back. The more he makes himself at home, the more out of place I feel.

'No, it's fine. You go ahead.'

Stig flashes me his dimples. 'I can save you my bathwater if you like.'

I frown, unsure whether he's being serious. Sharing water with family is one thing, but not with a complete stranger.

Stig grins. 'Only joking! We Norwegians do that sometimes. Joke, I mean.'

Ignoring him, I glance at the kitchen. It's nearly three in the afternoon. The toast we had this morning has long gone. 'I'll start dinner, I guess.'

'Great, I'm starving!'

'Who said anything about making *you* dinner?'

Stig looks hurt, and not play-acting hurt.

'I thought you Norwegians liked a joke?' I say, trying to sound upbeat.

He raises his eyebrows, then turns on his heel with a grin.

Bending down, I open a cupboard and grab an onion, a few potatoes and a cabbage. Yrsa was right, the place is well stocked. I take some bread from the freezer, ready for later, then start on dinner. I'm halfway through peeling a potato when I hear the water run. The cabin has never had good soundproofing – it didn't seem a problem before, but now the idea of using the toilet knowing I can be heard in the next room makes me cringe.

I hear singing. Badly and in Norwegian. I shake my head but can't help smiling as Stig's voice builds to a death-metal crescendo. I don't know the song, but it sounds like he's murdering it. Just when I think he's finished, a series of wails assaults my ears. As he returns to the deep-throated chorus, I grab a knife and find myself chopping in time with the tune.

Something darts past the window. The knife slips and I gasp as it slices my flesh. Sucking my finger, I wipe away the steam from the cooking and peer outside, but there's only fog. It's so dense I *can't* have seen anything.

Even though I'm unable to see the tree, I know it's there – why do I feel like it's watching me? I yank the curtain shut. There's something rotten about that tree. I can feel it emanating in waves.

I tear off a piece of kitchen roll and wrap it around my finger, pressing hard against the throb of pain. Blood oozes and spreads across the tissue, making it more red than white. Mormor must keep plasters around here somewhere. I open a drawer to find a stack of papers and riffle through them. Bills and shopping lists. No plasters, and no envelope with my name on it either.

I pull open another drawer and start to rummage, when Stig strides into the room dripping water.

'*Vannet er iskaldt!*'

'Sorry, what?'

He's wearing a towel around his middle. His wet hair hangs over his shoulders and his smooth chest is covered with a film of tiny bubbles. I turn away, then glance back at his muscular legs. I may be half blind, but even I don't need Kelly to tell me he's hot.

Stig seems unconcerned by the fact he's almost naked, which only makes it more awkward. Resisting the temptation to look at him, I stare at my throbbing finger.

'*Helvete!* What happened to you?'

'Oh, nothing. Just slipped with the knife.'

Stig gestures to a chair and I dutifully sit while he searches the dresser.

'I think I saw . . . Wait, I remember.' He pulls out a green box from behind a row of cookery books and I tut. Of course, I should have asked him to begin with.

Stig reaches for my hand and heat floods every part of my body; this must be how it feels to blush down to your toes. I pull away, but he grabs my finger and inspects the damage, informing me of what I already know – *it's a deep cut* – before smoothing on a plaster.

'You OK? Maybe you should lie down.'

I stand and turn back to the chopping board, doing my best not to look at his bare chest. 'See. Perfectly fine,' I say, snatching up the knife and stabbing an unsuspecting potato.

I don't know whether I'm irritated with him for wandering around half naked, or with myself for being bothered by it. As I bring the knife down, I can feel his eyes on the back of my head.

I risk a glance over my shoulder. 'Anyway, what's up with you? Did you forget the words to the song?'

Stig gives an awkward laugh. 'Oh, you heard that? Sorry, I didn't mean to be, er . . .' He frowns as if he's trying to think of the word. 'Insensitive.'

'It's OK,' I mumble. I liked hearing him sing. Though

his voice sounded dreadful, it made the cabin feel less empty.

'I got out because the water turned cold.'

Strange. It shouldn't run out *that* quickly. I put the dinner in the oven, then head to the bathroom. Stig follows me as I step into the steam and turn on the bath tap. The water warms my fingers instantly. 'Feels hot to me.'

Stig's black socks drip water over the side of the deep wooden tub. Mum used to complain it was like showering in an oversized barrel, but I loved sitting in there as a child, pretending I was voyaging the high seas in my own little boat.

Stig holds his finger under the tap and frowns. 'The lights were flickering too, but they seem OK now.' His face is so close to mine I don't know where to look. For a horrible moment I think he's staring at my eye – but he isn't. He's looking at my mouth. I turn the tap off and start to walk away, somehow managing to trip over my feet in the process.

Stig grips the towel at his waist. 'You must have a magic touch.'

If only he knew. His black shirt and slashed jeans hang on the back of the door, and I can't help wondering what they might tell me. I think back to his coat in the woodshed. How can he feel love and sadness and at the same time be consumed by such jealousy and hate? If I run my fingers over his jeans, maybe they'll show me a memory. I *want* to touch them. The realisation gives me butterflies.

I step towards his clothes, then stop. Wouldn't it be nicer if he told me, if we just got to know each other the normal way?

Stig coughs and looks at me expectantly. It takes me a moment to realise why. I glance at the floor. 'Sorry, right, I'll leave you to it,' I mutter.

As I turn to leave, I notice a blurred, misshapen face in the mirror. He must have drawn the sad hollow eyes and gaping mouth in the condensation. I think about remarking on his artwork, but when I look back the image has gone. The only monstrous face is mine.

I take my time in the shower, letting the warm water wash away the strangeness of the day, then change and towel my hair.

Stig is kneeling by the stove, feeding a log to the fire. He's brushed his hair and applied fresh eyeliner. Instead of the usual black, he's wearing a white shirt with ruffles down the front. There are no creases in it, so I guess he must know where Mormor keeps the iron. The boy is either incredibly nosey and likes poking around other people's houses, or he's been here for longer than he said. The thought brings me out in goosebumps.

Stig glances up with a grin and my fear evaporates. He hasn't done anything to make me doubt him. I'm being overly suspicious. 'Something smells good,' he says. For a second I think he means me, then instantly feel stupid.

I enter the kitchen to find the table set, complete with wine glasses, napkins and candles. He's even used one of Mormor's best tablecloths. Feeling underdressed in my grey jogging bottoms, I drag my fingers through my damp hair, wishing I had blow-dried it. *Stop it*, I tell myself. *You can't do anything about your face, so what's the point of worrying about your hair?*

Gandalf is curled up in his basket, head on his paws. 'Feeling better now, boy?' His ears prick up at the sound of my voice. I kneel down and pat his head, and he licks my face in return. That's the good thing about animals: they love you for who you are, not how you look. He stares at the door as if he's trying to tell me something. 'What is it?' I whisper, but he only lowers his head with a sigh.

Stig's right, dinner does smell good. Grabbing a tea towel from the rail, I open the oven and take out the casserole. Mormor was the one who taught me to cook. Not that I made much in London; it was something we did together. Disappointment tugs at my heart as I remember that we'll never do it again.

Stig sees my face and gives me a sad, knowing smile. He grabs some oranges from the fruit bowl on the dresser, then starts to juggle. 'What do you think? Good enough for the circus?'

I try to sound impressed. 'Not bad.' I know he's trying to cheer me up and that Mormor would want me to be happy, but it feels wrong to have fun without her. Like it feels wrong to be using her best tablecloth and wine glasses.

Stig's oranges tumble to the ground. I reach out and grab one, then knock my head on the table.

'You OK?' Stig crouches down and I move away from him without thinking.

'I'm fine,' I snap, annoyed with myself for being so clumsy.

Stig picks up the oranges, then stands and takes a banana from the bowl. He threatens me with it. 'Do you know what the Swedish think Norwegians call a banana?'

I shrug.

'*Gulbøy*. It means, yellow bend.'

'Really?'

Stig laughs. 'Yes, really,' and starts to juggle again.

I watch the fruit whizz in circles, then lay the plates on the table. 'Let me guess – fruit salad for dessert?'

Stig grins. 'I tried juggling custard but it got messy.'

We sit at the table and smile shyly at one another. Stig clears his throat and I wonder if he feels as awkward as I do.

'So you don't speak any Norwegian?' he asks.

I pick up my spoon and feel a pang of regret. At the time, it didn't seem worth learning a new language when we only came out for summer holidays.

'Mormor wanted to teach me, but no. I wish I did.'

'I can teach you a few words, if you like.'

'OK.' I try the casserole, which tastes just how I remember: rich and meaty mutton with cabbage and peppercorns, and a dash of cumin for warmth.

'So, where did you learn to juggle?' I ask.

71

'My ex-girlfriend was an acrobat.' A shadow of sadness passes over his face. He opens the bottle of red wine on the table and his expression changes as quickly as it came. 'Nina went to the same school as me, but her parents worked for a circus in Oslo. I watched them train sometimes – trapeze, high wire, contortion, that kind of thing.'

I nod along. 'Sounds cool.' But how would I know? I've spent months making jewellery in my bedroom with only a handsaw and metal for company.

Stig pours me a glass of wine, then fills his own and raises it. 'To making the best of things.'

My fingers caress the stem of the glass. Red wine always goes straight to my head, but I guess a little won't hurt. I raise my glass and clink it to his.

'*Skål!*' Stig drains his drink in one gulp.

I narrow my eyes, wondering if he's trying to get drunk. The thought of his coat nags at me. Maybe someone with an alcohol problem would be like two different people – maybe he gets angry when he's had a drink.

'*Skål,*' I say, and swallow my unease down with the wine.

'See, you're learning already,' he smiles. 'So, any plans for tomorrow?'

Get through each hour without being overwhelmed by grief or creeped out by a tree – but I'm guessing that's not the answer he's looking for.

Stig refills his glass. 'Maybe we can walk to the sea?'

We could be on holiday, the way he talks. Surely

72

he must have plans to go back to school or whatever he does? I take a sip of wine and consider asking, but what if he thinks I'm trying to get rid of him and takes offence? My only real plan is to turn the cabin upside down. The more I think about it, the more convinced I am that Mormor would have left me a letter.

'Actually I was planning to sort through Mormor's things.'

Stig lowers his gaze, abashed. 'Sure, sure. Of course.'

'Anyway, Yrsa said we should stay near the cabin.'

'Oh, that? Northern superstition. Like I said, it's probably just a stray dog.'

I nod, but Yrsa doesn't strike me as the nervous type. And they must be properly worried or why go to the trouble of buying a gun? I should tell Stig that I saw something outside the window earlier. I open my mouth, but he speaks first.

'I'm glad you turned up. I was getting bored of boiled potatoes.'

My spoon clatters to my plate.

Stig swallows hard. 'I'm sorry, that was a stupid thing to say.'

Suddenly it's like the first time we sat opposite each other, after I brought him in from the woodshed. What am I doing playing house with the boy who broke into Mormor's cabin? Cooking him a meal and using her best tablecloth and drinking her wine! I shovel casserole into my mouth. It burns, but not enough to melt the ice in my belly.

Stig lays his palms on the table. 'You have been so kind to me and I never said thank you.' His face is flushed from the wine. 'Seriously, you didn't have to lie for me. I want you to know that I appreciate it. Really.'

I nod and feel the tightness in my shoulders relax a little. I hadn't realised until now, but I've been waiting for him to say those words. Stig holds my gaze. 'I would have frozen to death if it weren't for you.'

My heart melts the tiniest bit. I guess things must be bad at home if he'd rather sleep in the woodshed than go back. 'Like a penguin lost in the snow?' I ask.

Stig laughs. 'Yeah. As cold as a penguin with no one to love me.'

I feel my cheeks burn and look away. Next to the sink is a pile of dirty pots and pans. 'You can make it up to me by doing the dishes,' I offer.

Stig grins. 'Sure, sure.'

'*And* make breakfast tomorrow.'

'No problem. For you, Miss Martha, extra-special pancakes!'

I take a sip of wine, enjoying the smoothness as it slips down my throat. We eat in comfortable silence; the only sound the hiss and crackle of the fire. When we're finished, Stig looks at me, his eyes startlingly blue. '*Takk for maten.*' He holds out a hand for my plate. 'It means, thanks for the food.'

'*Takk for maten,*' I repeat, liking the taste of the Norwegian words on my tongue.

Stig looks pleased. '*Det var deilig.* It was lovely,' he adds.

Gandalf whines at the front door and I feel my body tense. Stig puts our plates by the sink. 'We could walk him on a lead if you like.'

'OK.'

A lead sounds better than Gandalf running off into the night, but I'd be happier if we didn't have to leave the cabin. Still, I guess he has to be walked.

Stig zips up his boots, then attaches Gandalf's lead and slides back the bolt. It's cold and damp, but the fog has nearly lifted. Dark clouds smother the sky so that the moon is a faint blurred halo. As I do up my coat, the thought of going near the tree makes my stomach turn. I can't face it, not after such a nice meal. 'I might stay here and watch, if that's OK?'

Gandalf charges down the steps towards a clump of grass. 'Sure!' shouts Stig, his arm waving wildly as he's pulled by the lead. Gandalf sniffs like a dog possessed, then lurches again, his nose close to the ground. I laugh as Stig is dragged around. I'm not sure who's taking who for a walk.

Stamping my feet against the cold, I watch as they jog past the woodshed to the rear of the cabin. Even with the light of the moon, they soon become shadowy shapes. The longer I stand on the porch, the less I like it. Maybe I should call them back. But it's only been a few minutes; Stig will think I'm silly. Besides, I can hear his voice complaining in Norwegian – they can't be far. I watch my breath hang on the air and peer into the gloom. There's something odd about the darkness. It doesn't feel as empty as it should.

A howl shatters the night. A terrible, guttural sound – on and on like it might never stop. My heart batters against my ribcage. 'Stig!' I scan the darkness and yell his name again, but the only thing I hear is Gandalf barking.

Another terrifying howl. What the hell *is* that? I've only ever heard a wolf howl in movies, but this is nothing like that.

Something races past me. Not a person, but the shadow of a person.

I spin around, my fists clenched. Another shadow flickers past my shoulder, and another. I turn around and more rush past me into the cabin – all of them on my left side. The side where I am blind.

WINTER BRINGS HARD CHOICES

'What do you think it was?' I ask.

Stig unclips Gandalf's lead, then kicks off his boots. 'A wolf – what else?' He sounds angry with me, or maybe he's annoyed with himself for thinking it was a dog. Either way, there's something in the harshness of his tone I don't like.

I pace the room, my mind a whirl. I can't see anything strange now, but there was something out there, moving in the darkness. I saw *things* rush into the cabin – yet how could that be? Since the accident I've had zero sight in my left eye. I cover my right eye with my hand just to be sure. Nothing. A severed ocular nerve is just that: severed. It *can't* heal itself.

I stop mid-stride and rest my hand on the sofa. In

the kitchen earlier, when I saw something move outside the window . . . And in the bathroom, when I saw that creepy face in the mirror . . . The window and the mirror were both on my left side. Why didn't I notice that before? The back of my neck prickles. I glance around the cabin and shiver. Whatever the shadows are, they're in here now.

Stig is leaning against the kitchen counter, his face clouded with concern. I walk over to him, but what can I say that won't make me sound insane? The room reminds me of the war photos I've seen in history lessons, where families were forced to abandon their homes and leave everything: food on the table, a child's shoe on the floor. I stack the dishes, grateful for something to do.

Thud.

Stig's head snaps up.

Thud. Thud. Thud.

A slow rhythmic noise, regular as a heartbeat. Coming from inside the cabin.

Gandalf wags his tail as if an old friend has come to visit. I glance at the living room and back to Stig. He shakes his head, warning me not to move.

'Where's it coming from?' I hiss.

Thud. Thud. Thud.

Stig takes a step then stops, his face pale. In between the knocking is a softer noise, like distant rushing water. I've heard the sound before, like it belongs here. Stig's fingers graze mine and my skin tingles at his touch. I pull away without thinking, then regret it.

The noise continues: a steady rhythmic thump. I

follow the sound and find Gandalf sitting outside Mormor's bedroom door. I swallow, my mouth dry.

Thud-*shhh*. Thud-*shhh*. Thud-*shhh*.

I nudge open the door and Stig reaches in and snaps on the light. We look inside, then at one another. My legs feel weak, but I make myself enter the room. The noise is coming from the huge oak wardrobe. Stig watches wide-eyed as I walk towards it. Holding my breath, I open the door. Next to a rack of clothes is Mormor's little spinning wheel.

Moving.

I touch it and it stops instantly. The silence that follows is unsettling.

Behind me Stig mutters, 'Fy *faen, det var ekkelt.*'

'What?'

'I said, that was creepy.' Stig hovers in the doorway as if afraid something might jump out of the closet. 'What made it move?'

I inspect the inside of the wardrobe. 'No idea.' There's nothing to fall on the wheel, and even if something did, it shouldn't have kept moving like that. My voice sounds calm but my stomach is twisting and turning, like a hole is opening up inside me.

Gandalf sits at my feet and whimpers. The sight of Mormor's clothes fills me with sadness too. The wardrobe smells of her: the rose perfume she wore, mixed with herbs and sunshine. I look at her bunad. When I was a child, I begged her to let me wear it. If I touch it now, maybe it will make me feel close to her.

I reach my hand towards the costume, when a ball

of red yarn drops to the floor. The air goes from my lungs. I watch in wonder as it slowly unravels towards my feet. Too scared to move, I freeze, waiting. When nothing else happens, I bend to retrieve it. The other end is caught in something under the spinning wheel: a wooden chest.

Luckily the spinning wheel isn't heavy. Stig watches wide-eyed as I place it on the rug and then peer back inside the wardrobe. The lid of the chest is carved with the pattern of a tree, its branches and roots intertwined and touching so that it makes a perfect circle. If it weren't for the leaves, you could turn it upside down and it would look the same. Between the roots sit three women. Their arms are raised and they're passing a cord between them. The one on the right holds a pair of shears in her lap.

I don't think I've seen the image before, yet it seems vaguely familiar. The lid of the chest won't budge. There's not enough room in the wardrobe for it to open; I'll have to lift it out. I wrap my arms around it and pull, but it barely shifts.

'Stig, can you help me?'

He walks slowly into the room.

Grabbing the box by one corner, I try to slide it out but clumsily drop it.

'*Nei, stoppe!* What are you doing?' He points to the spinning wheel. 'Put it back!'

'It's OK. Something in the wardrobe must have fallen on it and made it move. I just need to get this chest out.'

He doesn't look convinced.

'We can do it together,' I offer.

Stig shakes his head. 'Not enough room. I can –' He heaves, then stops and tries again. Finally he manages to lift it. *"Helvete, det er tungt!"*

'What?'

'I said, it's heavy!' Stig groans and the chest drops with a bang.

'Thanks.'

He looks at me expectantly, as if he's waiting for me to open it.

'I'm OK now, thanks. I'll probably just go to bed.'

Stig looks at the box suspiciously, then reluctantly leaves the room.

The lid is heavy and creaks as I lift it. Like Stig, Gandalf seems keen to know what's inside. I nudge his head away and he licks my face. 'I know, boy, I want to see too.'

It smells ancient – of mothballs and mildew. Inside are dozens of neatly stacked books, canvas bags and rolls of material. On top of the pile is an envelope with my name on it. My breath quickens as I run my finger over Mormor's familiar handwriting.

My Dearest Marta,

If you are reading this letter, then I will have already gone. You will be sad, I know, but please don't waste your tears on me, little one. I have lived the life that was meant for me, and none of us can ask for more.

I have loved you since the day you were born, and it

has been an honour to watch you grow into the fine young woman you are. But a life cannot be made up of summers - and winter brings with it hard choices.

Inside this chest is your inheritance. Your mother barely stirred from slumber when it was given to her, but you, my child, are awake.

You wrote to me asking why you can sense things from touching people's clothes. I replied, but as I kept receiving letters, I can only presume mine did not reach you! The gift is one that I share also, as does your mother - though she refuses to accept it.

The story is a long one, and I hope you will learn Norwegian and read the journals for yourself. For now, all you need to know is that our ancestor, a weaver woman named Aslaug, made a sacred vow that she and her line would take care of the tree in the garden.

This has been the way for more than a thousand years. Once I am gone, the duty should fall to your mother, but I fear it will come to you. Every morning you must take water from the well and put it on the roots inside the largest chamber of the tree. I beg of you, this you must do. There have been many seers in our family, and I pray that the worst does not come to pass.

If you choose to look inside this chest there may be danger ahead - for our path is one of growth through hardship. But know that dozens of women have walked this way before you, women whose blood runs in your veins. Remember, the tree is the start of the journey and the end. Tend to it every day and listen with an open heart!

May the gods watch over you and keep you safe.
Until we meet again,
Your loving Mormor x

Scrawled at the bottom is:

The gift of reading clothing lies dormant until you meet the Norns. For we have a very special destiny - and I believe they appear to wake us to our fate.

I feared your mother would never accept the truth, so I took you out to the tree many times, hoping you were ready to see them. Perhaps I should have told you sooner, but I promised your mother I would not - and I couldn't risk her never bringing you to the island again. I made the mistake of pushing her too hard, I see that now. I am so sorry for what is to come. I hope you can forgive me.

Mormor had the same ability as me, and so does Mum? My pulse races with my thoughts. Who or what are the Norns? I haven't seen them! Mormor took me out to the tree the day before the accident, but I didn't hear anything.

I read her words for the third time. Of course Mormor hid the letter in the wardrobe, knowing I would be drawn to touch her clothes. The moving spinning wheel and the wool dropping to the floor, do they mean her ghost is with me now? I look around and shiver. I can't help feeling that there's something in the room, watching me.

I look back at the letter. Part of me wants to forget I ever found it. Mormor makes it sound so important, but the idea of going near the tree fills me with dread. I study her shaky handwriting. If Mormor wrote it on her deathbed, maybe she wasn't in her right mind.

I move towards the chest and Gandalf tilts his head, his brown eyes full of concern. He barks and twitches a grey eyebrow, and I stroke his ears. 'It's what I came here for,' I say. Sitting on my knees, I look inside. Even if it means hardship and danger, I haven't come this far to close the lid.

I KNOW NOTHING ABOUT HIM

There are dozens of books inside: ancient dusty tomes bound in dark brown leather, shiny hardback notebooks and rolls of mouldy-smelling paper – not to mention piles of canvas bags and folded linen. I don't know where to begin.

The light flickers as I randomly select a notebook. Inside is tiny black handwriting, like an ant dipped in ink has crawled across its pages. I turn to the front: on the first page is written 'Karina, 27 februar, 1918'. Beneath it is a black and white image of the same severe-looking woman I saw in the photo on the shelf. My great-grandmother. Her long wavy hair is parted in the centre and there are dark circles under her eyes. I search the pages, hungry for clues, but there are no more photos, and the Norwegian words mean nothing to me.

Placing the book down, I reach for a roll of paper. I slide off the red velvet ribbon, and the paper curls up on itself, not wanting to share its secrets. Written at the top is 'Solveig, 6 oktober, 1886'. Different handwriting, this time written in verse – again in a language I don't understand.

I pull some parchment aside and find a sheet of charcoal sketches. A huge hooded figure in a tattered robe sits on a throne. Where there should be a face is only blackness. The next sheet shows the tree with shadowy figures, all with shoulders slumped and heads bowed. Each of them looks in a different direction, seemingly unaware of the others. Something about it makes me feel terribly lonely. I put the drawing to one side, hoping that Solveig might have been inspired to draw something more cheerful.

No such luck. The next drawing shows a man hanging upside down from one of the tree's branches. His feet are bound together, and one of his legs is bent outwards. In the distance, two ravens fly around him. His arms reach down to the ground, his finger touching a pool of water. In the ripples are symbols I don't recognise.

I look at the next page and my stomach drops. It shows the tree and a hideous, grinning creature with a skull for a head. Bulging eyes stare out of its face and it has long, matted black hair. It crawls on all fours, looking out from the page. More disturbing is what lies beneath it. Dozens of human faces are piled together in the earth, as if they're in a burial mound. My throat tightens. The picture reminds me of Mormor's stories about *draugr* – walking corpses who come back to kill the living.

The light bulb fizzes and flickers. I am gathering up the papers, wanting nothing more to do with them, when the room goes dark. Heart racing, I rush to the door, Gandalf following at my heel.

In the lounge Stig is sprawled across the sofa, a roaring fire in the stove. His leather coat lies on the floor, its arms spread wide like it's marking a crime scene. At first, I think he's passed out, but his eyes are open. The brandy bottle at his feet is nearly empty. He has an annoying habit of helping himself.

'You OK?' I ask.

Stig startles. 'You made me jump!' He gives a nervous laugh. 'The spinning wheel just now – that was a bit creepy.'

I shrug, not wanting to talk about it, and he sits up and moves to one side. For a moment I wonder if he's expecting me to sit next to him. I rest a hand on the back of the sofa and glance at the kitchen. The washing-up has been done; the room is spotless.

'I came to get a lamp. I think the electricity is on the blink.'

'The blink?'

'It means about to stop working.'

The light bulb overhead burns without a flicker, and Stig raises an eyebrow.

'I couldn't sleep either, after Dad died.'

'Oh, I'm sorry. I didn't know.'

'Why would you?'

I feel my face flush. I guess he's right; I don't know anything about him.

Stig gestures for me to sit by him but I shake my head, not wanting to touch his clothes. He frowns and turns away with a shrug. Worried I've offended him, I perch on the edge of the sofa.

He stares at the fire. 'People say grief gets easier with time, like you've got the flu. No one says it hurts like a punch to the stomach.'

Sadness stings my eyes. Losing Mormor *does* feel like someone has punched me. I feel so sore inside I don't know if I'll ever heal.

My voice is barely a whisper. 'And does it get easier – with time?'

Stig shrugs. 'The first few days were the worst. I had these nightmares, really weird stuff. Dad wasn't the easiest person to live with, but after he went . . . I don't know. I had so many things I wanted to say and suddenly it was too late. I was angry, I guess.'

He forces a smile. 'Every day is different, but, yes, it does get easier. Now I only think about the good times we had together. That way, remembering doesn't hurt so much.'

I want to believe him, but thinking about the happy holidays I had with Mormor makes me miss her even more. Not wanting to talk about myself, I ask a question instead.

'Your dad – how long ago was it?'

'Six months.'

He picks up the coat from the floor and holds it on his lap. 'This was his. It was the only thing I took of his, after he died.' I think back to when I touched the coat in the woodshed, and how it seemed to have a split personality. Of course, it makes sense. I *was* reading the emotions of two different people.

Stig points to the elbow of one sleeve. 'That burnt patch is from when we went camping last year. A log from the fire rolled on it.' He shows me the beige lining. 'And there, that dark circle is a petrol stain. I know because it happened when I was helping him fix his motorbike.'

Stig bunches the worn black leather between his hands. His voice is thick with emotion. 'He wore the coat every day. He was wearing it when . . .'

'How did he die?' I ask.

Stig's face darkens.

'Sorry, it's none of my business.'

He swallows hard. 'A car crash.'

'Oh. I'm sorry.'

Stig mutters, 'It's me who should be sorry,' then takes a deep breath. 'When I wear his coat, it's like he hasn't really gone. After it first happened, part of me thought that if I kept the coat, he might come back for it. Stupid, I know.'

Before I can say anything, he kneels in front of the stove. The door gives a tiny squeak as he opens it. He pokes at the logs, though the flames already burn brightly.

'It doesn't sound stupid,' I say.

He smiles shyly. 'Sorry, I don't know why I'm telling you this.'

A waterfall of words rushes through my head. I wrote to Mormor about my ability, but that's not the same as having someone to actually talk to about it. My chest flushes with excitement. I glance at Stig, wondering how much I dare to tell him.

'I think clothes can hold memories,' I venture.

Stig nods. 'You may be right. I like clothes with missing buttons and stray threads. It means they have a story to tell. The same with people.'

I shift my weight on the arm of the sofa. 'You like people with missing buttons?'

Stig laughs. 'No. I mean that people who aren't perfect are always the most interesting.' I remember the first time he saw me. Stig looked terrified, but not because of my eye. He hasn't looked strangely at it or asked me about it once.

He pulls his phone from his pocket. 'Look at this for crazy clothes.' I take it and see goths in amazing outfits: a guy in a top hat with long feathers trailing down the back and a woman with lots of tattoos in a tight corset. I stop when I come to a girl with short black hair, balanced on a trapeze wire, and blowing a kiss to the camera. Stig's acrobatic ex, I presume. She's wearing bright red lipstick and is stunning. I hand back the phone. Maybe he was trying to make me feel better, but I feel worse. There's no point pretending. Someone like Stig is never going to want to keep a photo of me – *the circus freak* – on his phone.

A distant howl sends a shiver down my spine. I glance at Stig and he looks back at me, his face pale. A loud bang makes us both jump.

Gandalf leaps from his bed and barks at the door, while Stig rushes to the window and pulls open the curtain. 'Sounded like a gunshot.' He cranes his neck. 'Not far away.'

I go over, but there's nothing to see – only darkness. 'It came from near the forest. That's where Yrsa and Olav live. Maybe it was Olav, shooting the wolf.'

Stig returns to the sofa and flops down, seemingly relieved. 'There was only one shot, so he must have got it.' I listen for a howl or a second gunshot, but the night returns to silence. I wish I shared Stig's optimism. Maybe Olav got whatever's out there – or maybe he missed and it got him. There's no way to know.

I stand for a few moments longer, then reach for an oil lamp on the dresser and take down a box of matches. 'Goodnight,' I say, and head to Mormor's room.

'*God natt*,' Stig calls. 'Sleep well.'

I open the bedroom door and freeze. The chest is where I left it, but the books are not. They're stacked in piles on the floor, as if waiting to be read. Fear lodges in my throat. I want to scream for Stig but I clasp a hand to my mouth. He was creeped out by the spinning wheel. What if he goes and leaves me here alone? Or worse, what if he thinks I'm seeing things or making it up? My jaw clenches as I carefully close the door.

I light the lamp with trembling fingers. Afraid to turn my back on the chest, I stand with it on my right side – where I can see it.

Nothing moves. The room is silent apart from the low moan of the wind.

I take the top book from the first pile and flick through words I don't comprehend. Why would anyone want me to look at books I can't understand? A twitch of movement in the chest catches my attention. I look inside to see a large roll of material and a single journal. On top of it is a canvas bag, embroidered with the letter K. Maybe I'm not meant to read the books; maybe I'm meant to find something else. The bag is still now. Perhaps it was just my imagination.

Afraid to go near it, I glance at the door. I wouldn't be brave enough to touch it if I was alone. But I'm not. Stig is here. I can call him if I need to.

Swallowing my fear, I reach inside and lift out the bag. The material is stained and tatty and smells of mothballs. Opening the string, I find a rag doll. I tip it onto the floor and it lands against the chest, head slumped on its body. Strands of yellow wool have been sewn on as hair, but are faded from age. Its arms and legs are basic: white material stuffed into lumpy shapes, roughly stitched together with black thread.

I take the journal from the chest and look inside to see the name Karina – my great-grandmother. Not wanting to touch the doll, I reach out with the book, planning to scoop it up and drop it back inside. Before I can touch it, the doll slips to one side. For a sickening moment, it seems to jerk its arm.

The face that gazes up at me is innocent enough: a red line for lips and a delicate nose. It has black cross-stitches for one eye, but the other is missing. I sit back on my heels, my heart beating sideways in my chest. Someone has unpicked the eye on the left side of its face.

WHY WOULD IT FOLLOW ME HERE?

I wake to the aroma of pancakes and fresh coffee. For a wonderful, fleeting moment everything is how it should be: Mormor is pottering about the kitchen, making breakfast. Then I remember and a fist squeezes my heart. I sit up, my head groggy as last night comes back to me. The chest is at the end of the bed, everything back inside and the lid closed.

Several journals lie open on the pillow next to me. I must have fallen asleep looking at them, though how I managed to sleep after what happened I don't know.

'*Nei*, Gandalf!' Stig's voice carries a note of laughter.

I throw a jumper over my pyjamas and brush my hair, then go to the bathroom. When I pad into the living room, Stig is in the kitchen, flipping a pancake.

His hair is tied back and the sleeves of his black woolly jumper are pushed up. Gandalf wags his tail and stares at the food flying above his head.

'*God morgen!*'

'What time is it?'

Stig switches off the gas burner, then turns to me with a grin. If he has a hangover, it doesn't show. 'Eleven. I heard you getting up, finally! Here we are – pancakes as promised.'

He sets a plate on the table and I pull out a chair. 'Great, thanks.'

I take a bite, but hardly taste it. The creepy doll and the books . . . it doesn't seem real. I don't even remember putting the rest of the journals back in the chest before I went to sleep.

I watch Stig sip his coffee. The spinning wheel moving, that was real. He heard it too. I want to tell him everything, but at the same time I'm not sure I should. Ever since the shadows rushed past me on the porch, I've had a strange sense of foreboding. Like in a dream, where there's something lurking on the edge of your vision but you're too afraid to look. Talking about it would mean having to admit there's something in the cabin with us – either that, or I am seeing things.

Worries flap inside my head, pecking at me like angry birds. Before she started her medication, Mum would stay up all night painting and then scream in terror. When I rushed into the room, the canvas would be covered in black paint – whatever horror she'd seen had been in her head. After the second time it

95

happened, Dad called the doctor out. She said Mum had been hallucinating. That's when the bottles of pills appeared in the bathroom cabinet.

'Notice anything different?' asks Stig.

I startle at his voice. The room seems normal, though it's odd he hasn't opened the curtains when it's light outside. Stig strides to the window and pulls back the curtain like a proud stage magician. The world outside is brilliant white.

'Snow?'

He beams like a kid at Christmas. 'Ja, snø – and lots of it!'

I take another bite of pancake and wash it down with coffee. It tastes less bitter this time. Stig must have remembered and mixed the grounds with egg. I do my best to smile, grateful that he's trying to make things nice for me.

Stig wipes the window. 'I haven't been out yet. I was waiting for you to get up.'

I glance at him over the edge of my cup.

'I wanted for us to share it together,' he explains.

This time I don't have to force a smile.

'More?' he asks.

What were the words he taught me last night? 'Takk for maten.'

Stig looks impressed. 'You remembered!'

He zips up his boots and grabs his coat from the sofa. 'Come on, let's go!'

I lower my cup and hesitate. I was hoping to show him the journals and ask him to translate, but I guess

96

it can wait. If I'm honest, part of me wants to forget about the creepy books and drawings and pretend last night didn't happen.

'Shouldn't I get dressed?'

'You look lovely, Miss Martha.'

'Are all Norwegians as mad as you?'

Stig laughs and raises an eyebrow.

'I'm not going out there like this! Wait a minute.'

I dash into the bedroom and pull on six layers of clothing. When I return, Stig is waiting by the front door, his coat buttoned up tight, and his scarf around his neck. He wears a hunting hat with fur along the edge and long flaps over the ears. It makes him look cute and cuddly, despite his leather coat and spiky boots.

I shrug into my coat and a warm feeling spreads through me as Stig lifts the hood over my head. 'Ready?' he asks. I nod and he opens the door to endless blue skies and acres of white. The world has been made new overnight. He bows and lets me go first. I'm glad he waited for me, so we could step into it together. I don't like to admit it, but Mum and Kelly were right – despite everything, it feels good not to be shut away in my room.

The snow squeaks and crunches under our boots as we walk down the steps. My foot slips and I grab the rail and pretend to admire the view as I steady myself. Stig races headlong into a field of white. He throws his arms wide and spins. 'I love snow!'

His enthusiasm is infectious. I jump into the craters

of his footsteps and laugh at Gandalf, who barks and chases his tail. I try a little spin, just to see how it feels. Stig grabs handfuls of snow and throws them into the air and Gandalf tries to catch them.

Stig's face is flushed pink and his eyes are as clear as the sky. Mormor would have loved this. She would have loved him.

'Hey, Martha, catch!'

I turn as he throws a snowball. It misses.

'You'll have to do better than that!' I shout.

I grab a handful of the white powder and pat it into a ball. When Stig reaches for more, I throw it and it hits him hard on the ear, much to his surprise and mine. 'Sorry!' I say, laughing.

Stig shakes his fist. 'Right!' He grabs some snow and rallies the troops – in this case Gandalf. 'You saw that, didn't you, boy?' I turn and squeal as a snowball sails over my head, quickly followed by another. I race away and Stig gives chase. Unable to get me, he stands and catches his breath.

I hold up my hands. 'Truce?' I offer.

Stig nods. 'But only because I'm a gentleman.'

I grin. 'Not because you can't catch me?'

Gandalf trots around the side of the cabin and we trudge behind him through snow half a metre deep. The view from here is even more stunning. The flat expanse of white stretches all the way to the forest without a single track, human or animal, to disfigure its cold perfection. If there is a wolf, it hasn't passed this way recently.

The branches of the fir trees bend under the weight of snow: fairy-tale queens in white fur coats, arms dripping with diamonds. Even the twisted tree looks less bleak with a sprinkling of winter white. Seeing it casts a shadow over my happiness. I don't want to go near it, but I can't let Mormor down. Once we're inside, I'll ask Stig to translate the journals; maybe they'll explain *why* I have to water it.

A raven caws and lands on a low branch, its blue-black body stark against the snow. It twitches its head and looks at me intently, then spreads its wings to reveal a clump of grey feathers on its chest. It looks just like the bird I saw when I got off the ferry at Skjebne, but why would it follow me here?

Stig is throwing snowballs and chasing after Gandalf. I nearly call out to him, but stop myself. He'd probably think I was making it up. I turn my back on the tree and walk away, but I'm convinced the raven is following my every move. A harsh caw makes me glance behind. Sure enough, it's watching me.

'Hey, Martha, is my nose still there?'

'What?'

Stig walks over and prods a finger to his face. 'I'm so cold I thought it had dropped off.'

I pull a face at his nonsense, and then bend to make another snowball. The raven swoops past my head and I duck away, afraid.

Stig chuckles. 'You're not afraid of birds, are you?'

'No, I just –'

The bird flies back to its branch and caws again.

I have the strangest feeling it's trying to tell me something.

'Come on – let's get inside before parts of me really do fall off!' says Stig.

I pull my gaze away from the tree and trudge after him. As we walk, a black shape flies overhead, trailing us like an ominous shadow.

THINGS PASSED DOWN IN THE FAMILY

My cheeks and nose tingle from the warmth of the cabin as I collect the journals, then drop them on the table. I'm glad we went for a walk together first; it makes it easier to ask Stig for a favour.

'So this is what you found in the chest last night?' Stig nudges one of the books with his finger, as if afraid to touch it.

'Uh-huh.' I stand over him and arrange them in the order I want them to be translated: Mormor's journal first, then Karina's and the books of sketches.

He picks up a random roll of paper and pulls at the ribbon. 'What are these? Legal documents or something?'

'No, journals and drawings. Things passed down in the family.'

Stig unrolls the paper and flattens it out, ignoring the books, and I sigh with annoyance. The picture is the one of the tree with the man hanging upside down. Beneath his head is a pool of water, with lots of symbols drawn inside.

'Hmm. Looks like Odin,' says Stig.

'Who?'

'The All-Father, the highest of the gods. The one the Vikings believed in. They believed in Odin, and Thor and Loki, and other gods. In the Norse myth, Odin hung himself from the world tree in search of knowledge, and the runes appeared in the well.'

I bend over the picture. 'Do you know what the symbols mean?'

Stig turns to me in surprise. 'You don't know? You're wearing one of them.'

I grasp the silver charm around my neck and my breath catches. I don't know why I fashioned the three interlocking triangles. The design just came to me.

'That's the *valknut*, Odin's symbol,' says Stig. My fingers squeeze the charm as Stig points at the other shapes on the drawing. 'You use the runes to tell someone's fate and for doing magic.'

Leaning over him, I grab another roll of paper and open it out. 'What about this?' It shows a giant figure wearing a hooded robe, seated on a throne.

'Hel, maybe – ruler of the underworld.' Stig sees my confused expression. 'The Christians stole her name and gave it to their idea of 'hell'. The Norse didn't believe in the devil; there's no fire or burning people.'

He frowns, then adds, 'The dark mother goddess, to whose cold embrace we must all return. It's said that when you die, Hel forces you to look at yourself.'

'What do you mean?'

'She makes you see the good and bad in yourself. I guess so that you can learn from your mistakes.'

He flicks through the sketches, seemingly puzzled. 'Did your grandmother do these drawings? Didn't she show them to you before?'

Ignoring the question, I sit opposite him and scrabble through sheets of paper. 'What about this one?' I ask, holding up a drawing of the tree with three women sitting at the base of its trunk. Like in the image carved on the chest, they're passing a cord between their hands and one holds a pair of shears. I tug anxiously at the charm around my neck as Stig studies the picture.

'The Norns,' he says.

My stomach does a tiny somersault. 'Are you sure?' The charm comes away in my hand with a snap. 'Damn.'

'It's OK. We can fix it.' Stig takes the necklace from my hand before I can stop him. 'We just need to –'

I snatch it back, annoyed. 'I know what I need to do. I made the thing!'

Stig sits back in his chair. He looks as if he's invited a stray cat into his house, only to discover it has fleas. I pick at the chain with my nail.

Stig points. 'It's that link there, see –'

'I'm not totally blind!' I snap. Feeling guilty, I mutter, 'It would help if I had some tools.'

Stig leans over and opens a drawer of the dresser, then hands me a little pair of pliers. For once, the fact he knows where everything is makes me smile. 'Thanks. I'm sorry. It's just – all this, it's a bit weird.'

Stig shrugs like it's no big deal and watches as I attack the chain. I've always had a steady hand, but not today, it seems.

'Can I?' He gestures for me to give him the pliers and the necklace.

I hand them to him reluctantly, and then peer over as he carefully opens the clasp. 'So, the Norns, are they gods too?' I ask.

Stig tucks a wayward strand of hair behind his ear, then deftly closes the silver link. 'No. They're older than the gods. They're the women who weave fate – they decide what kind of life we have and when we die.'

That must be what Mormor meant when she said the gift of reading clothing lies dormant until the Norns appear to you. She was talking figuratively about fate. A tiny laugh escapes me. How could I have thought otherwise? 'So the Norns aren't real women?'

He gives me a quizzical look. 'Depends. Some people believe the Norns and the old gods are real. There's a name for their religion, but I don't remember what it's called.'

He drops the chain on the table and takes his phone

from his pocket. 'I keep forgetting there's no Internet. I could have looked it up for you.'

I try to put on the necklace, but I can't quite open the clasp.

'Here, let me.'

Stig stands up and walks around the table. I lift up my hair, feeling self-conscious, and he carefully lays the chain around my neck. His fingers lightly brush my skin and I tingle at his touch. He closes the clasp, but doesn't move. 'So you've inherited all this?' he asks.

'I've inherited more than that,' I sigh.

Stig sits opposite me and waits for me to explain.

'Mormor tended to the tree every morning and she wants me to do the same.'

'Tend?'

'It means to look after.'

'I know what it means. But how do you look after a tree? Doesn't it look after itself?'

I pick up Karina's journal and flick through it until I come to a sketch of a woman kneeling inside the tree. There's a wooden pail on the ground next to her. 'I need to take water from the well every morning and put it on the roots inside the biggest chamber of the tree.'

Stig takes the journal from me and scans the page. 'But your grandmother didn't really believe what it says here, did she?'

I tut, unable to hide my irritation. 'I don't *know* what it says!'

'Of course, sorry.' He drops the book on the table,

as if something bad has just crawled from its pages, then glances at the window and back to me. 'According to whoever wrote that, the tree out there is *Yggdrasil* – the world tree.'

'The one you said Odin hung from?'

Stig pulls the band from his hair and it tumbles over his shoulders in a great black mane. 'Yes, the tree at the centre of the cosmos. It connects the worlds: its branches hold the realm of the gods, and beneath its roots is the underworld. It's where the Norns live.'

My head throbs. Believing in destiny is one thing, but surely Mormor didn't actually think there are women who weave fate living in the tree outside? Stig flicks through the book and reads, 'Each day, Odin's ravens Huginn and Muninn fly through the nine worlds, then perch on his shoulders and whisper their findings to him. Such was his thirst for knowledge, Odin plucked out his eye to be granted a drink from the well of wisdom.'

The pit of my stomach turns cold. 'Wait. Odin only had one eye?'

Stig nods and carries on. 'When the Norns would not tell him the secrets of fate, he hung himself from the tree. At last he spied the runes in the well, and in them found the answers he sought.' I nod for him to continue. 'Listen to this . . . The sagas speak the truth when they tell how Odin hung for nine days and nights. And it is true that neither food nor water would he take. But what they do not tell is how a young weaver woman watched over him. After he cut himself down from the tree with a cry, she took him to her cabin and gave him mead and the comforts of her bed. From Aslaug did spring a line of earthly daughters –'

'Hang on. Mormor said I had to water the tree because someone called Aslaug made a sacred vow more than a thousand years ago.'

Stig glances at me quizzically, then back at the book. 'It says here that because Odin hung from the tree, it caused its decay to quicken – so he tasked Aslaug and her descendants to water it from the well to preserve its life.'

I stand and go to the window. The branches of the tree shiver violently in the wind; it seems more alive than ever. Surely it's nonsense; some kind of hoax. I can't really be descended from an ancient Norse god.

I stare at the tree, trying to untangle the knot of thoughts in my head. A black shape flies at me. I jump as it crashes into the window then disappears, leaving a smudge on the glass. I grip the counter with both hands, my knuckles white.

'Fy *faen!*'

Stig grabs his coat. For a moment my legs forget how to move. Then I push my feet into my boots and rush after him, my feet slipping on the cabin steps.

Breathing hard, I trudge to the garden and see a black shape in the snow. A raven.

'Is it . . . ?'

Stig shrugs. 'I don't know.'

It's the same bird as before, I know it is. A beady

black eye blinks and stares, closes and blinks again. Crouching next to it, I reach out my hand. I don't know what to do, but I have to do something.

It gets to its feet, flaps awkwardly a little way, then lands on the snow. Perhaps it's injured. I give chase and it takes to the air, then lands and does the same thing again. Finally it settles on a low branch of the twisted tree. It caws and caws, its eyes burning into me with murderous intensity – and this time I know what I have to do.

TIME IS RUNNING OUT

'What do you mean, it wanted you to follow it? You don't look well, Martha. Please, just sit down a minute.'

Stig watches from the door as I scrabble under the kitchen sink. I shove a bottle of paraffin oil to one side and sweep some sponges to the floor. At last I find it: a large wooden pail.

Stig inhales sharply when he sees it. 'This thing about the tree – it's just a story. Make-believe.'

Ignoring him, I march down the steps and around the side of the cabin.

He follows close behind. 'Don't you think you're –'

'What?' I snap.

His long black coat flutters about his ankles like a

raven that's forgotten how to fly. He pauses, a bewildered look on his face. 'Well, taking it too seriously.'

The pail knocks against my leg as I walk. 'And the raven?'

He hurries after me, breathing hard. 'Birds do that. They get caught in a gust of wind or lose their way. Just because a raven hits the window doesn't mean Odin sent it. It doesn't mean that you're his descendant!'

I spin around, suddenly angry. 'You know nothing about me, or my family!'

'I know you miss your grandmother. And I know grief can make people crazy, but –'

'I'm crazy? That's what you're saying?' I throw the words at him, then stomp away.

'*Nei, vent!* Please, stop!'

I march towards the tree. Maybe it's all in my head, but I'm sure the raven was trying to tell me something. It *wanted* me to go to the tree. I shouldn't have waited; I should have done as Mormor asked and watered it straight away.

Stig calls, 'Why don't we go inside? It's freezing out here. You can do it tomorrow.'

I pause and turn with a heavy sigh. 'I know it seems weird, but I need to do this.'

We stand for a long moment, staring at one another. Emotions play across his face, like the way the contours of a landscape go light and dark when a cloud passes overhead. His eyes are wild and destructive. Stormy sea eyes that could drag me under if I let them.

I frown, wishing he would say something that would

allow me to explain, but how can I, when I don't understand myself? Our breath hangs in the space where words should be.

Eventually he turns away, muttering in Norwegian. I watch him trudge back to the cabin, his shoulders slumped like he's one of the figures in the drawings. He disappears inside and loneliness settles over me like a tattered cloak.

I stare at the frigid sky and sigh. I didn't tell Stig about the books that moved by themselves or the doll twitching, because he probably wouldn't have believed me. I know he could never fancy me, but I don't want him to think I'm losing my mind.

Taking a shuddery breath, I turn to face the tree. Buzzing fills the air, getting louder with each step I take. I hold my arm against my nose, but it doesn't stop the hideous smell. Mormor died over a week ago and no one has tended to the tree since. She didn't say what would happen if no one watered it, but it can't be good.

I walk around the tree, my boots tripping over gnarled roots. The well is small, three people could join hands and reach around it, but something tells me it's unfathomably deep. I dip the pail into the water and a raven launches from a branch, its black wings clapping in applause. I watch it fly away, my mind a blizzard of questions. Mormor fed a raven on the porch every day, and swore it was the same bird that came back to her. Maybe it *has* been watching me.

A gust of wind shakes the branches and snowmelt

111

drips down my neck, making me shiver. The thought of the wolf stalks my mind. What if Olav didn't shoot it? What if it's still out here? I glance around, feeling vulnerable.

The buzzing is louder now. Something bad is going to happen, I can feel it. Bending almost double, I enter the largest chamber. The hole is bigger than before. Too black and too deep, it gapes like an open mouth jeering at me. The wood around it is scored with deep lines, as if an animal has tried to get inside, or something has clawed its way out. Instinct tells me to throw the water at the hole. Closing my eyes, I picture Mormor: her long blonde hair and her mischievous grin. It gives me the strength I need. The buzzing roar is so loud it hurts. I press my hands to my ears and the pail thuds to the ground. It's like the hole doesn't want me to get near.

Gritting my teeth, I snatch it up and chuck the water at the tree's roots. It hisses like a fire being put out and there's a horrible sound, like the drawn-out gasp of a thousand souls taking their final breath. My skin prickles. What would make that noise?

I rush out and trip on a root, landing head first in snow. Mist snakes around the tree and wraps around my body. I scramble to my feet and two ravens explode from a branch, making my heart lurch. I look for the cabin but the world is falling away.

Confused, I stumble against the moss-covered trunk. What did Mormor say? *Listen with an open heart.* Swallowing hard, I press my ear to the tree. Time slows as a steady drumbeat sounds inside. Wood creaks and groans, like something is stirring deep within. I hold my breath and listen. I've heard that sound before . . .

The bark splits open and green smells invade my nose. I stare in disbelief as a forehead pushes its way out of the tree: a woman's face with chiselled cheek-bones and a sharp, pointed chin. Moss and dirt tumble from her eyelids as she blinks into life.

Her head snaps towards me with a sickening crack. Unable to move, I watch as a gnarled knot opens into a perfect hole, revealing a pale worm curled inside. Her voice sounds like wind through the dead leaves of a tree. 'Time is running out, Marta.'

JUST LEAVE NOW

Stig is throwing a log on the stove when I stagger in through the door. He looks up in surprise as I lurch towards him. My legs tremble so much, I can barely walk.

'*Helvete!* What happened to you?'

My breath is quick and shallow. 'Mormor,' I croak. 'Get Mormor.' And then I remember. I feel so sad and tired I could dissolve into a puddle of my own tears. I slump onto the sofa and close my eyes.

Stig stands over me. 'What was it? Did you see the wolf?'

I shake my head. 'No. There was a woman – in the tree. She said –'

'You're in shock, Martha. You need to get warm.'

Stig shakes my shoulders, his voice insistent. 'Come on. You need to get out of those wet things.'

Groaning, I fumble for the zip of my coat but my fingers are numb and useless. I open my eyes and see him leaning over me. His face is different, or maybe I'm seeing him properly for the first time. He has stubble on his chin, and the crease in his bottom lip seems even deeper, more kissable. My eyes close as I imagine his mouth pressing against mine.

'Wake up, Martha!'

Stig tugs at my coat, yanking me out of my fantasy. I twist my head to the sofa, feeling ashamed. Of course Stig doesn't want to kiss me. No boy wants to kiss me. Stig pulls my arm from the sleeve of my coat and tries to haul me up. He's so close I can feel the heat from his body. Any closer and his jumper will touch me. I can't bear to know what he thinks of me right now.

'I can do it. No, don't,' I wail. 'Just let me do it. You can't let your clothes touch me!'

Stig holds up his hands, a confused look on his face. 'OK, OK.'

I clumsily shrug out of my coat, and it slides to the floor with a heavy, wet slap. My neck and chest are oddly clammy, as if there's something worse than wet fabric clinging to me. The woman in the tree – Mormor said the ability always lies dormant until the Norns wake you to your fate. But I haven't . . .

Suddenly I remember. That's why I fell! I was in the garden and I heard Mum and Mormor arguing. I climbed the tree because I wanted to eavesdrop, when a face pushed its way out of the bark. The same face I saw just now. That's what made me lose my grip and fall. Is the face one of them? Can the Norns be real?

Stig kneels by my feet and gently tugs at my boots, his eyes full of concern. The room dips and sways, making me dizzy.

'I'm going to get you a blanket. While I'm gone, take your trousers off.'

I tug at my wet jeans but they're superglued to my legs. Panting with exertion, I eventually manage to wriggle free. Stig reappears holding a colourful crocheted blanket and a pile of my clothes. He glances at my bare legs and swallows, a pained look on his face. He places the sweatshirt and bottoms on the sofa. 'Here, put these on. I'll make you a hot drink.'

I look at my feeble white thighs, hating the paleness of my skin. Stig hands me the blanket and I cover myself with it. He hesitates, as if he doesn't want to leave but doesn't know what to say. Eventually he pulls his gaze away and goes to the kitchen.

Once his back is turned, I peel off my damp top. The thought of him seeing me in my underwear makes me shiver. Part of me wants him to see, wants him to notice my body. But then I glance down at my dingy bra. Everything about me is ugly.

I pull on the dry clothes, then wrap the blanket around my shoulders and reach my hands towards the fire. The heat slowly thaws my flesh, making my fingers throb and leaving a meltwater of thoughts pooled in my brain. All those nights I lay awake, trying to under-stand why clothes speak to me. I thought that if I could just talk to Mormor, then maybe I would understand. Now that I know the truth I feel trapped. I want to do as Mormor asks, but I hate the thought of going near the tree – and whatever weird entity is inside it – again.

Gandalf rests his chin on my knee and looks at me with sad, knowing eyes. 'You knew it was a bad idea, didn't you?' I whisper. He twitches an eyebrow. That damned chest. I should have nailed it shut and caught the first flight back to London. I didn't ask for this – any of it. *Time is running out* – what the hell is that supposed to mean?

Stig appears and places a steaming cup of coffee in my hands. I sip it and brandy burns the back of my throat, making me cough. He adjusts the blanket around my shoulders.

'Better now?'

I nod, then blow on my drink, embarrassed and confused by the emotions tumbling inside me. I love how Stig makes me feel cared for, but maybe he's only being friendly or is just grateful to be here. I peek at his face and see him studying me. He looks as puzzled as I feel. 'Did you fall in the snow?' he asks.

I drain the last of my drink and mumble, 'Yes. No. I don't know.'

He takes the cup from my hand. 'Well, something happened. Come on.'

I want to tell him, but where do I start? 'You wouldn't believe me,' I say.

He sits next to me and places my cup on the floor, then turns and peers into my good eye. 'Try me.'

I think about the woman's face in the tree and my teeth start to chatter.

'You're still cold. Look at you!' Stig rubs both of my arms, then tries to pull me to him.

I flinch away, and then stare longingly at his chest. I want so much to be held by him, but his jumper . . . I couldn't bear it if he doesn't believe me.

Stig drops his arm, a hint of hurt on his face. I bite my thumbnail, annoyed with myself. 'Stig? I'm sorry, it's just that . . .'

He glances up hopefully, but I don't know how to finish the sentence. I close my mouth, afraid to speak in case I cry.

Stig twists to face me on the sofa. Most people see my eye and stare or look away, but he holds my gaze without blinking. He smiles at me and my stomach flutters.

'You said something just now, about not letting my clothes touch you.' Stig grabs the hem of his black jumper and pulls it to his nose. The grey sweatshirt he wears underneath is frayed at the edges. He sniffs his shoulder. 'Is it because I smell? I haven't done any laundry for a while.'

I don't know whether to laugh or cry. 'It's not that.'

Stig flashes me his dimples. Suddenly his face becomes sombre. He lowers his voice. 'I promise not to judge. Whatever it is, you can tell me.'

I pick at my fingernails as the words drip out. 'Things

have been happening to me. I can do things, weird things I haven't told anyone about. And I can see things.'

Stig takes a moment. 'O-kaay. What kind of weird things?'

'The weird kind, only weirder.'

'Stranger than strange?'

I give a tiny nod and he tucks his hair behind his ears. 'Is it to do with the Norns? You said something about a woman in the tree.'

A tear slides down my face. Stig pulls me to him and I fall against his chest. As soon as the wool touches my cheek, feelings and memories flood my mind. His jumper is riddled with regret. Stig blames himself for the death of his father. He had phoned him at two in the morning, claiming to be stranded after a party, but he didn't really need a lift. His mum had been stopping them seeing each other, and Stig just wanted to talk. When his father didn't show up, Stig walked home in the rain, hating him. The next morning, the police knocked on the door. His dad's car had been found wrapped around a lamp post.

Stig pretends to be this happy-go-lucky person, but inside there is so much anger and sadness and self-loathing. He uses humour to mask his pain. Why hadn't I seen that before? He strokes my hair tenderly, and I wish I could take away the hurt. I force my thoughts away from the emotions in his jumper and breathe in his smell: shampoo mixed with wood smoke and the faintest odour of sweat. His body is so warm and solid I don't want to leave his side.

He says in a soft whisper, 'Tell me everything. I'm big enough and ugly enough to take it. That's what you English say, isn't it?'

'You're hardly ugly.' Just looking at him makes my pulse quicken. Kelly used to go through magazines and rip out photos of boys, then put them together to create her ultimate man. I would laugh and call it her ultimate Frankenstein. I never really liked the clean-cut American guys she went for – and I still don't know if I'm into heavy metal and black clothes; I just like Stig. Maybe if he fancied cheerleaders and prom queens I would feel differently about him, but he's into girls with piercings and weird clothes and tattoos, girls who are different.

I lay my head against his chest, wanting to share myself with him even though it scares me. 'I fell from the tree outside a few months ago. That's how my eye happened.'

Stig presses his hand to my head but doesn't say anything. I keep talking, afraid I will never say it if I don't get the words out now. 'It started in the hospital. I can tell things about people by touching their clothes, like their memories and emotions are trapped in the material.'

I swallow and add, 'I thought Mormor would be able to explain it. That's why I came.'

Suddenly I get a different emotion from Stig's jumper. Fear and disbelief. I knew it was too good to be true!

He tries to make his voice sound calm. 'So you think the journals are right?'

I can't stop. He already thinks I'm crazy; what have I got to lose? Besides, I will burst if I don't tell someone. 'Outside just now, I saw a woman's face in the tree. I think it was one of the Norns.' I look down at my hands, hating how insane I must sound.

Stig speaks cautiously. 'Maybe there's another explanation. People with hypothermia sometimes see things. If you fell, maybe the cold made you . . .'

I snatch back my hand. Stig reaches to grab it and the sleeve of his jumper brushes my arm. A new wave of guilt washes over me. Stig was so angry with his dad, but then, after he died, he felt guilty for feeling that way. He would give anything to talk to him again.

I speak without thinking. 'You know, you shouldn't feel bad about phoning your dad that night. Your mum didn't make it easy for you to see each other, and you only wanted to spend some time with him. You couldn't have known he'd crash into a lamp post.'

Stig leaps to his feet, his eyes wide. 'How did . . . ? I never told you that!'

I pick a stray thread from my sleeve. I had to make him believe me somehow, but what if I've made things worse?

'Martha?'

I point to his jumper.

'You know all that just from touching my clothes?'

'I didn't mean to, but when you pulled me to you just now –'

Stig presses a hand to his head. 'When you said . . . I didn't know. I mean, that's amazing!'

He perches on the arm of the sofa. 'What else do you know?'

'Just how guilty you feel. I could probably feel more of your emotions if I sat with it for longer. I'd say it's thirty per cent cashmere, seventy per cent wool. I'd have to touch something made from cotton to get more facts.'

Stig looks down at his jeans. 'Wait, so you're telling me you get different things from different kinds of material? My jeans might tell you something different to my jumper?'

I nod.

He shakes his head and starts to undo the buttons of his jeans, revealing the tops of his black boxer shorts. I blink in shock.

'So if I need to keep a secret from you, I'd better get naked!' He laughs, then does his jeans back up. 'Seriously, that's amazing. Like, wow-amazing.'

He takes off one of his black socks and dangles it before me. 'Here, try this!'

I shove his arm away. 'No, thanks!'

He sniffs it and winkles his nose. 'I wouldn't be surprised if that one talked!'

I never thought I would laugh about it, but suddenly it seems so funny. Stig wobbles on the arm of the sofa as he tries to put the sock back on. He laughs so much he nearly falls off.

He stops and looks at me wide-eyed, his voice serious. 'If the journals are right and you are descended from Odin, I mean, wow! Odin is the most powerful of the gods, the All-Father! Who knows what else you can do?'

A flicker of excitement catches inside me. I guess having some of his power *would* be amazing.

Stig grins. 'You have to tell me more! Is it just clothes, or could you read the material on this sofa because I just sat there?'

'No, it's just clothes. I'm not sure why. Maybe it's something to do with intent, because they're made to fit us or something.'

'Clothes are an expression of who we are on the inside, you mean?'

Before I can answer, he fires more questions at me. 'I have to know – are my jeans annoyed because I don't wash them enough? And my shirt, is it cross because I don't iron it?'

I shake my head and giggle. 'It doesn't work like that!'

Stig pretends to hit me with his sock. 'Well, it should!'

My phone vibrates in my jeans pocket. I'm still laughing when I swipe the screen. Twenty missed calls and eight text messages. My heart races. Most are from Mum, some from Kelly and Dad.

Stig looks over. 'Something wrong?'

'I'm not sure.'

I read through the most recent messages.

Dad: *Please call me darling, it's important x*

Mum: *Where are you? I know you're not with your dad. Call me ASAP*

Kelly: *Sorry!!!!! Your mum was worried sick. Like having a panic attack. I had to tell her. Please don't be mad!!*

My chest tightens. Mum knows I'm here. She knows I lied to her. I bite my lip, worried what she's going to say. I read the final message and my stomach drops.

Mum: *I don't want to scare you, but you need to leave the cabin. I'm getting the first flight I can. Go to Olav's house. Go anywhere. Just leave NOW.*

A Dark Shape on the Ground

'It's Mum. She knows I'm here. She says to leave the cabin.'

I show Stig my phone.

'What? Why?' He scrolls through the messages. 'She sent this a couple of hours ago. Even if she got the first flight . . .'

My throat tightens. 'The last ferry goes at five fifteen. She won't get here until tomorrow now.'

I read the messages again, a knot of anger in my chest along with something else – an empty, dull ache. I miss her. When I was a kid, I only had to graze my knee and Mum would come running. Despite everything, I know she loves me and would do anything to protect me – I felt it when I touched her jacket in the hospital. I wish she was here now to keep me safe.

Stig goes to the window and peers out. 'Why does she want us to leave? Did you tell her you saw a face in the tree?'

'No.' But could she know something?

Stig's face is pale. 'How far is Olav's house?'

'Two or three miles. There's a path that cuts through the forest; if we go while it's still light I can easily find the way.'

'There's no one closer?'

I shake my head and swallow, my mouth suddenly dry. We haven't heard a howl since the gunshot last night, but what if Olav didn't kill the wolf?

Stig pulls on his boots. 'I think I saw some snow-shoes in the woodshed.'

The overhead light in the kitchen makes a buzzing sound, then flickers and goes out. Stig stares at it, then back to me. His voice is edged with fear. 'I think we should go, Martha.'

I look about the room and a sense of dread crawls across my skin. Ever since I saw the shadows rush past me on the porch, I keep feeling there's something in the cabin with us. When the spinning wheel moved by itself, Stig was properly freaked out. Maybe he senses it too – that feeling of being watched.

I bite my lip. I want to get away from this place, but I don't know if we should risk going outside. The electricity often plays up – it doesn't have to *mean* anything – and the living-room light hasn't gone out.

I pick up my phone. 'Let me try calling Mum first, OK?'

Stig nods and reaches for his coat while I dial her number. I hold my breath and wait. She speaks and my heart leaps, but it's just a recording telling me to leave a message.

'Mum, it's me. I'm at the cabin. Mormor is dead, but you know that. Why didn't you tell me?' My voice wavers. 'You need to come quickly – something's happened to the tree. I can see things, and . . . Mum, why do we need to leave?' I hear Stig repeatedly pressing the kitchen light switch and look over at him. 'I'm not here on my own. We're going to walk to Olav and Yrsa's now, before it gets dark. Please hurry, Mum. I'm scared.'

The phone bleeps and a voice asks if I want to re-record my message. I hang up and return the phone to my pocket with a sigh.

'Stig, maybe we should stay. We don't know why she sent the message. If she knew about the wolf, maybe she wouldn't want us to go outside.'

He frowns. 'We only heard one shot fired last night. So Olav must have got it first time, otherwise he would have fired again.' He pauses, then adds, 'A wolf would only attack if it was hungry, and there are plenty of sheep to kill out there.'

I stand up and reach for my boots. 'I guess.' Stig might be right, but even without a wolf, I don't like the idea of going anywhere near the tree again. Gandalf yawns and stretches as I shrug into my coat – at least one of us is looking forward to a walk. I grab the torch from the dresser and change the batteries. While my back is turned, I hear the cutlery drawer open and glance around to see Stig wrapping a knife in a tea towel. When I bend to clip on Gandalf's lead, he shoves it in his coat pocket.

Stig opens the door and yellow light spills onto the porch. My cheeks and nose tingle from the cold. I pull on my hat and gloves, then step down, my boots crunching on snow. Beyond are acres of white under a grey-blanket sky – enough light to see by, but for how long? Stig jogs to the woodshed and I breathe into my gloved hands, trying not to think about the shadows that rushed past me last night.

A few minutes later Stig returns, carrying some snowshoes. He drops two of the elongated tennis racquets before me and I step into them and fumble with the straps. I lift one foot and take a wide step, careful not to hit the other. They're cumbersome but at least I won't sink into the snow.

Stig strides out like an expert. 'You'll soon get used to them.'

I take a few clumsy steps after him, then look over my shoulder. Thin grey smoke rises from the chimney, snaking into the pale watery sky. It feels wrong to abandon the cabin with the living-room light blazing, but if Olav and Yrsa aren't there we'll need to find our way back in the dark.

No, Skjebne isn't exactly known for its nightlife, so where else would they be? We'll soon be at Olav and

Yrsa's, facing the inquisition. Mum will arrive in the morning and take me home. As much as I don't want to go near the tree, I can't help worrying that I've let Mormor down. She begged me to water it – and now I'm turning my back on it, the same as Mum did.

I watch Stig trudge along the edge of the garden and hurry after him, though the snowshoes make it impossible to do anything but shuffle. Ignoring the twisted tree, I focus on the dark forest ahead. My lack of depth perception makes it hard to judge distances, but luckily I know this garden and these woods like the back of my hand. I've played in them every summer of my life; even at home in London, my dreams would bring me here.

The only sound is the wind and the muffled crunch of our footsteps. Something moves to my left. I turn to the tree and gasp. Dozens of little children hang from its branches. I scream and Stig stops. 'What is it?' he calls.

Fear closes my throat. It's not children hanging from the tree, just their empty coats. I focus and realise I'm wrong. The tree is covered with scraps of material, fluttering on the breeze. It reminds me of the nightmare I had about Mormor – snatching at a piece of cloth on the tree. Sadness stabs at my heart. I blink and the branches are bare.

Stig searches my face. 'You OK?'

I take a deep breath and wave my hand. 'I'm fine. Just keep going!' My legs ache from the weight of the snowshoes and taking such wide steps, but I don't want to rest. The sooner we get to Olav and Yrsa's, the better.

At the edge of the fir trees, Stig stops and waits for directions. I peer into the dark forest, hoping I can find the way. Luckily I soon spot the start of the path.

'There.' I point. 'We need to go for about a mile, I reckon.'

Gandalf growls and sniffs at the ground and Stig touches my arm in warning. We freeze and look at one another. Once we enter the forest, it will be harder to move quickly. If there is a wolf, we won't stand a chance. We hold our breath and listen. High above us, the tops of the trees sway wildly in the wind, making a constant rushing sound. The full moon is growing bright in the darkening sky. We need to keep moving.

Pushing away a heavy spruce branch, I step into the forest. Sheltered from the cry of the wind, it's eerily quiet: just the crunch of twigs beneath our feet, the swish of fir, and the occasional *whhump-whhump* of snow sliding from branches.

Touching the tree trunks with my gloved hands, I lead the way, with Stig and Gandalf close behind. The lower parts of the trees are covered with hundreds of tiny thin branches, which add to the gloom. Dead and spiky, they reach out like skeletal fingers, threatening to slash at our faces. The torch is heavy in my pocket and it's a comfort to know it's there, but I don't use it. Better to let my sight adjust to the moonlight. After ten minutes or so, Gandalf stops and growls at a patch of undergrowth. My skin prickles. I stare in every direction. Nothing but fir trees and the watching eyes of a raven.

By the time we emerge from the forest, the moon is high in the sky and half hidden by cloud. Olav and Yrsa's place sits on a hill in the distance, its lights twinkling. My heart leaps with joy.

'Good, they're home!' shouts Stig. We grin at one another and walk a little faster. We'll have some explaining to do when we get there, but I don't mind. My nose and toes are numb; I just want to get out of the cold.

Gandalf barks and charges off, tugging the lead from Stig's hand. I stomp after him, while Stig huffs and flaps his arms in annoyance. Gandalf zigzags through the snow, back the way we came. Whatever scent he's picked up, he's not letting it go. 'Not now, Gandalf! Come back!' Olav and Yrsa's house is only fifteen minutes away, less if we hurry.

A dark shape stalks out from the shadows of the trees and my body stiffens. It's just Gandalf. I breathe a sigh of relief and chase clumsily after him. He's got something in his mouth: a pale padded glove. I take it from him and an image of Mormor flashes into my mind, clutching Yrsa's gloved hand and begging her to water the tree. Tears ache in my throat as I remember the anguish she felt. The material starts to show me something else. Something terrible . . . slashing black claws and . . .

Stig takes the glove from me and the connection is lost.

'What's that?' He turns it over to reveal a stain on the cuff.

Gandalf paws and whimpers at something a little way off. Stig gives me an anxious glance, then pulls the tea towel from his pocket. It falls to the ground and the blade of the knife gleams. Holding it out, he walks forward. I follow, my heart pounding. Gandalf is standing over a dark shape on the ground. It looks like a person, but it can't be.

'*Faen!*' Stig grabs me and tries to hold my head against his shoulder, but I pull away. Olav's grey beard is frozen, his mouth open. His arms lie stiffly over his body, holding a gun. My gut clenches. I think I'm going to be sick.

Stig goes closer and mutters in Norwegian, then whispers, 'His neck has been slashed.' I turn to look away, a taste of bile in my mouth, and see another shape in the snow. Just ten paces to my right. My heart drops to my stomach. Please, no. It can't be.

Stig grabs my hand and squeezes tight. We walk over together. Yrsa's huge sheepskin coat is shrouded with frost, her frozen face covered in blood. A flap of skin hangs loosely from her cheek. I cover my mouth with my hand. The sleeves of her coat have been torn to shreds, the material drenched in blood. Beneath her, the snow is stained dark.

A sob rises in my throat. 'Stig, what do we do?'

He stares blankly, then gestures to the house. 'Olav has a car. Come on, it's not far!'

Wiping away tears, I clamber after him.

A howl rips through the night. Coming from Olav and Yrsa's house.

Stig's face is stricken with panic. 'We have to go back! *Run!*'

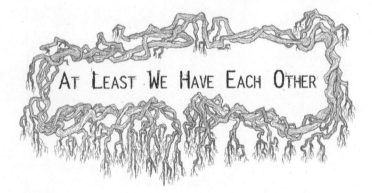

At Least We Have Each Other

Stig hurries down the hill towards the forest. The snowshoes are impossibly heavy – I *can't* run. The wooden frames catch on each other and I fall into a snowdrift.

'Stig, wait!'

I try to get up, but my foot hits my other leg and I thud back down. My heart thumps in my chest. I take a deep breath and am about to yell again when a furry face nudges my neck. Gandalf licks my nose and I cry with relief. Holding onto his body for support, I stand and then stagger down the hill.

Stig is waiting at the edge of the forest. 'You OK?'

I rush into the trees – 'Yes. Come on!' – but it's so dark I can't find the way. I grab the torch from my pocket and my fingers fumble with the button. Stig bites off one of his gloves and switches it on for me. I sweep with the beam, but all I see are densely packed tree trunks. At last I find the path.

'This way!' I call.

Even with the torch and the light of the moon, I can barely see the trees three metres ahead. I rush forward and a spiky branch slashes my cheek. I yelp and raise my arm.

Stig follows behind, his breathing heavy.

Another distant howl.

'Quick, Martha!'

I swallow a sob, wishing I could run, but the stupid snowshoes! Olav and Yrsa were badly clawed but not eaten, so it doesn't kill for food, whatever it is. Every snapping twig sends a jolt of fear through me. What if it's got our scent? There's no way we can outrun it!

When we emerge from the forest, both of us are panting hard. Mormor's cabin blazes brightly in the dark.

'Come on!' urges Stig.

I snatch a few deep breaths, then trudge towards it.

We're almost at the garden when Gandalf turns back and barks.

Something is moving through the forest behind us, breaking and splintering wood.

I chase after Stig, panic forcing speed into my legs. Gandalf could easily streak ahead, but he stays close. He growls at the darkness behind me, but I don't stop, not even to catch my breath.

Stig charges onto the porch and rips open the cabin door. I clamber up the steps, not pausing to take off my snowshoes, and fall inside with Gandalf just behind. Sprawled on the floor, I desperately gulp at air.

Stig bolts the door, then kneels and puts his arms around me. There is so much fear and anguish in his coat. I bury my face in his neck. 'What *was* that?' My shoulders heave with sobs. 'Poor Olav and Yrsa!'

'We're safe now, Martha. It's OK. It's OK.'

He helps me to the sofa and I collapse onto it, my limbs aching and frozen. He takes off his snowshoes, then pulls off mine. I can't get the image of them out of my mind. Something had clawed Yrsa to shreds. I glance up, and Stig looks as sick as I feel.

'We have to tell someone, the police or –' He takes his phone from his pocket and mutters angrily in Norwegian, then shoves it back. I check my phone but there's nothing. No new messages and no signal.

Stig goes to the window and yanks the curtain shut. He stands with his back to me for a moment. When he speaks, his voice is strained but strangely calm. 'Your mother will be here in the morning. I'm guessing she'll bring a car. We just have to get through the night.'

A couple of hours ago he was desperate to leave the cabin, but now he knows something is out there. Now he's seen what it can do . . .

Stig kneels before the stove and opens the door. I watch as he pokes the fire then takes a log from the basket. How can he carry on as normal?

I chew my thumbnail and whisper, 'You said it was a stray dog.'

He gives me a hurt look.

A tear runs down my face. 'You said Olav had shot the wolf.'

He says nothing.

'They were *clawed* to death! Not bitten. What kind of wolf would do that?'

He shrugs and shakes his head sadly. 'I don't know.'

Yrsa seemed so strong – mentally and physically. The way her arms were ripped, she must have put up a fight. They had a gun but they still couldn't stop it.

I clamp a hand to my mouth as I remember.

Stig frowns. 'What is it?'

The raspy voice when I got off the ferry . . . it sounded like the woman in the tree.

'No bullet can stop the dead.' I say the words quietly, almost to myself.

'What?'

'There are claw marks around the hole in the tree. Like something crawled its way out. You said the tree's roots reach down to the underworld.'

'What are you saying?'

The shadows that darted past the kitchen window and then rushed by me on the porch; the creepy face in the mirror . . . The Norns were trying to warn me! Mormor must have known what would happen if the tree wasn't watered. She didn't say, because it was too hideous.

'The tree is rotting because no one watered it, and now the dead are escaping.'

Stig's face is ashen. 'You can't be serious.'

I step into the dark kitchen and light an oil lamp. The journals and drawings are spread over the table, where we left them. I search through the sketches frantically, then gasp when I find it. The creature with a skull for a head and long matted black hair, crawling over a burial mound of faces. It has huge black claws – the kind that could make those marks around the tree and slash Yrsa to shreds.

Stig follows me and stands at my elbow. 'You're saying something like that crawled out of the tree, and that's what killed them?'

I point to the creature's claws. 'A *draugr*.' Just saying the name turns my insides to ice. 'Mormor told me about the dead that return. I thought they were just stories.'

Stig grabs the drawing and turns it over. 'Stop this. You're making it worse. We don't know what's out there. We just have to stay inside and –'

'And what? We'll be OK?' I snatch up some journals. 'One of these books has to talk about the *draugr*. Maybe it says how to get rid of it.' I flick through their pages. 'We have to know what's out there, we have to know what it's capable of, we have to know what it –'

Stig grabs my arm. 'Breathe, Martha.'

I gulp a lungful of air but it doesn't lessen my panic. Stig looks at the journals and for a moment I think he's going to read them. Instead he gestures to the sofa. 'Sit down. I'll make us something to eat.'

'Eat?!' I clutch the books to me. 'I can't eat now!'

'You need your strength. You haven't had a thing since breakfast.'

My arms tremble and several journals drop to the floor. He's right. I need to get a grip. Stig is doing his best to look after me. I feel bad for what I said just now. He couldn't have known that this would happen.

He turns his back to me and places the oil lamp on the kitchen counter, then picks up a loaf of bread. A surge of loneliness makes me want to hug him.

'Stig?' He glances over his shoulder, his eyes more beautiful than ever in the half-light. I muster my best Norwegian accent. '*Du er deilig.*'

He raises his eyebrows. 'You just said I'm delicious.'

My cheeks burn. 'I did? I meant to say you're lovely. I mean, for looking after me.'

He looks startled at the compliment. He coughs, his face flushed, then mutters, '*Takk,*' and turns away.

I feel stupid. Why did I say that? I pick up the fallen journals and grasp them tightly, wishing I had kept quiet. Maybe I should go and sit on the sofa; whatever I say will only make it worse. But I don't. I gaze at Stig as he slices the bread, watching the movement of his shoulders and the way his hair falls down his back.

A shadow shifts: behind the dresser, in the corner. My throat closes. The darkness is moving, expanding and deflating, like an animal breathing. I watch transfixed, then take several hasty steps back into the living room. The shadows around the dresser are paler now, but the edges of the lounge seem darker, as if whatever it is has crawled along the wall to follow me. I bump into the edge of the sofa, then drop onto it, the books tumbling from my grasp.

Hugging my knees to my chest, I bury my face in my hands. Something nudges me and I nearly jump out of my skin. Stig hands me a plate of sandwiches and puts two cups on the floor. He flops down next to me, then leans over and takes a sandwich from my lap.

I glance behind the sofa. The shadows are moving again – this time by the kitchen table. Stig turns his head to follow my gaze, but then goes back to eating. He doesn't seem to notice anything. I'm glad. Whatever's in here with us, it's not like we can go anywhere. I just have to hope it leaves us alone.

We chew in silence. The only sounds are the hiss and crackle of the fire and the wail of the wind. The journals sit between us on the sofa. Stig glares at them. 'I think we should burn them.'

I put my hand on them protectively. Despite everything, they are part of my inheritance, part of me. 'What if they talk about the *draugr*? Shouldn't we find out?'

He shoves the books and they fall to the floor. 'Can't we talk about something else?'

'Like what?'

'Anything! Anything else.'

There are dark circles under his eyes where his

eyeliner has smudged. Maybe he wants to talk because *he* needs to take his mind off things.

'OK, what do you want to know?' I sigh.

Stig sips his coffee. 'I don't know – what do you like doing?'

I shift in my seat, feeling slightly uncomfortable. 'I make stuff out of metal.'

'Great, what kind of stuff?'

I think back to my room and my brooches and necklaces.

'Jewellery. Spiders and ravens.'

He raises his eyebrows.

I take out my phone and scroll through some photos until I come to a silver pendant shaped like a raven. Stig reaches for the phone and I show it to him, feeling shy.

'You made that?'

'Yup.'

'Wow! That's amazing.'

He flicks through more photos, seemingly impressed. 'Who is this?' I reach for my phone and there's a tiny spark of electricity as our fingers touch. I wonder if he notices it too, but his face tells me nothing.

'My friend Kelly.'

'And this guy?'

It's a selfie of Darren and me. I took it at his Halloween party, before the accident. He's dressed as a zombie and is wearing white face paint which covers the worst of his acne. I'm a witch, holding a broomstick made from twigs.

'Darren. My friend's cousin.' I shrug and take my phone. 'No one important.'

'Really? He seems to like you.'

I glance back to the photo. Darren's arm is draped around my shoulder, reaching for the broomstick. I vaguely remember him making a joke, saying I could ride him any time.

'You look good together.'

I give a tiny shrug. Now I've met Stig, my thing with Darren seems so trivial. Darren made me laugh, but there is something special about Stig. Just being in the same room as him is exciting. When he's near, I want to pull him close. The way he looks at me sometimes, I get this warm shiver. Darren never made me feel like that.

Stig gives me a quizzical look and I study the photo again. 'We look ridiculous. Someone set my broomstick on fire with a candle halfway through the night, and Darren . . . Well, he's not going to be interested in me now.'

Stig huffs. 'I bet guys hit on you all the time. You just don't notice.'

I frown, hoping he isn't making fun of me. 'I'm blind to it, you mean?'

He glances at me over the rim of his cup. If he notices the bitterness in my voice, he doesn't show it.

'Anyway, what happened with your girlfriend, the trapeze artist?'

Stig takes a bite of sandwich, then another. He chews thoughtfully.

'The girl you showed me on your phone, that was her? She looks beautiful.'

Stig nods and narrows his eyes, as if he's not sure what to make of that. 'I guess so.'

'What happened between you?'

He shifts slightly in his seat. 'I went through a bad time after Dad. And Nina is the kind of girl who likes things to be fun.'

Something flickers in the corner of my eye: a shadow near the front door. I sense it moving closer, and have the feeling that we're being watched.

Stig sighs. 'We had this huge argument, and then she fell . . .'

'She fell?'

'From the trapeze wire. They said her harness wasn't done up properly.'

'Oh no. Is she OK?'

'Her mother phoned me from the hospital. She was in a coma.' He notices my worried expression and adds, 'It's OK. She woke up the next morning. She's fine.'

'So, did you finish with her, or . . . ?'

Stig's eyes flash dark. 'Nina was the one who ended it. She met someone else.' A hint of pain passes over his face, but he forces a smile. 'Someone who made her laugh – a clown.'

I stifle a laugh. 'Really?'

Stig grins. 'No, not really. She fell in love with the lion tamer.'

I smile, despite the awfulness of everything, and our

eyes meet. His face is soft in the glow of the fire. For a moment I almost forget Yrsa and Olav – but the image of their frozen faces is right there, just behind my eyelids.

Stig gives me a sideways glance. 'So what about you? Not found your lion tamer yet?'

The room is suddenly hot. I shove the blanket off my legs. 'Something like that.'

He puts the plate on the floor, then takes off his coat and lays it on the sofa. I think about the different emotions I felt when I touched it . . . there was such anger and jealousy.

'Stig, can I ask about your dad?'

'Sure.' He seems a little surprised, but doesn't sound defensive.

'You said you came to Skjebne with him?'

'Yes. We came just after Mum threw him out. It was great, mostly. We went hiking and fishing every afternoon, once his hangover had worn off. He told me about the dreams he'd had when he was younger, before he got married and had a kid.'

'Like what?'

Stig's face brightens, as if thinking about it makes him happy. 'Travel, build a boat. I remember we saw this old building for sale by the harbour. We talked about doing it up and turning it into a guesthouse.'

'But you never did?'

Stig gives a hollow laugh. 'The place is still for sale. It was good to dream though. I thought if we started something out here together, he might stop drinking.

I don't know – it felt like a somewhere we could be happy.'

It's strange to think that Stig must have been on the island at the same time as me. I might have passed him and his dad out walking. I gaze into the fire, remembering. 'I had the best summers here too. Dad would come out as well sometimes, when he wasn't working. He used to call Mormor an *outrageous eccentric* and they'd play practical jokes on each other. Back then, even Mum would laugh and join in. I remember this one time, Mormor woke me up in the middle of the night just to have a picnic in the midnight sun.'

'She sounds like fun.'

'She was.'

A log shifts in the stove and our words die down with the flames.

Stig's voice is quiet. 'I didn't say before, but when I overheard the women at the harbour talking about this place being empty, I felt I had to come.'

I wait for him to go on.

'It was like my feet brought me here, without my knowing why. When I got to the cabin, I felt so bad about my Dad dying, and losing my money, I sat on the doorstep and cried.'

I reach a hand to his, but he tucks his hair behind his ears before our fingers meet.

'It was strange, but the door was open, like the cabin wanted me to come in.'

It would have been just like Mormor to invite him inside. I take a trembling breath and Stig looks mortified.

'Sorry, that was the wrong thing to say.'

'No, it's not that. So what made you run away?'

He places his cup on the floor. 'After Dad died, Mum let stupid Erik move in. He was always nagging me to get a haircut and wipe the mess off my face. He talked about Dad like he was some loser – like he was an angry drunk and we were lucky to be rid of him. We'd argue and Mum always took Erik's side.'

His face is shadowed in anger. 'One day I found Dad's coat in the dustbin. It was covered in herring and potato peelings. Mum knew what it meant to me, and she let Erik throw it away. I didn't have a plan; I just left and found myself here.'

'And then I showed up.'

'Yeah!' Stig laughs. 'Then you showed up and it was terrifying!'

I lean back and cross my arms. 'I look that scary, do I?'

He shakes his head and smiles. 'The way you pointed your phone at me like it was a gun. And the way you yelled. Yes, you were scary!'

His voice becomes serious. 'I felt so bad telling you about your grandmother.'

I hadn't thought about it before, but it can't have been easy for Stig either. I do my best to lighten the mood. 'And then I threw you out and left you to freeze in the woodshed.'

'I was lucky you let me stay!'

I gesture to the journals. 'Lucky? Are you sure about that?'

'That . . . not so much. But being with you is nice.'

I rest my head on his shoulder and gaze at the fire. His jumper holds fear and worry but there is content-ment too. He enjoys my company and feels at home with me. A feeling of warmth spreads through my chest. I tug at the threads with my mind, wanting to find out more, but the harder I try, the more they evade me. It's almost as if I want to know *too* badly. I give up with a sigh. If he does like me as more than just a friend, it is hidden deep.

I snuggle closer to him and tell myself that everything will be OK. Mum will arrive in the morning. We just have to get through the night, like Stig says. I try not to think about the shadows in the corner of the room. Whatever's there can't be worse than what's outside, and at least we have each other.

Stig strokes my hair for a few minutes, and then his hand drops to his side. A yawn escapes me and I close my eyes.

When I wake, the room is dark. The electric light in the living room must have packed up too. The flames in the stove have died to nothing; the only light is the red glow of the logs. Gandalf is growling softly in the back of his throat. I shiver and rub my arms, then lean over the back of the sofa to see what he's looking at. He wags his tail and I shush him quiet.

The wind has dropped and the cabin is eerily quiet,

almost as if it's holding its breath, waiting for something to happen. I glance at the door. With any luck, whatever was out there is miles away by now, but even so, the idea of a creature roaming the blackness . . . I don't want to think about it.

Gandalf growls again, louder this time. What's got into him? I call his name softly, trying not to wake Stig, then reach out to pat him on the head. He backs away from me, his hackles raised. I follow his gaze and then I see it too – staring down at me from the ceiling.

A Horde of Desperate Faces

A forlorn face with dark eyes and long wavy hair peers down from the shadows. My breath stops in my chest and goose pimples prick my arms. I cry out and Stig wakes with a start. I point and he looks upward. The shadows gather into the shape of a woman's torso. Below that they trail into threads of nothing, like a rag doll that's been ripped apart.

Stig shakes his head and looks confused. He doesn't see it. I press my palm to my left eye and the ceiling looks normal. When I take my hand away, the shadows congeal. The head twists and two dark eyes lock onto mine. I gasp and grab Stig's arm.

'Martha, what is it? What's there?'

'A face in the shadows,' I whisper.

'*Faen.*'

'It's watching us,' I hiss.

Stig jumps up from the sofa and tries the light switch – nothing. None of the lights are working. He grabs the torch from the dresser. 'Where is it now?' he asks, aiming the beam at the ceiling. The woman glares at me and opens her mouth in a silent scream. Stig shines the torch on her and the shadows scatter like cockroaches.

My shoulders drop with relief. 'It's gone.'

'Are you sure?'

I glance around the room, my heart thudding, but there's nothing. No weird movements and no scary face. 'The light must have chased it away.'

A low growl makes us both startle. Gandalf is staring fixedly at the wood stove, the fur on his back bristling. My voice sounds small and forced. 'Hey, what is it, boy?' Gandalf gives a slight twitch of his tail but doesn't turn to face me.

There's another face, in the stove door. As if someone's trapped inside, looking out. It starts to disappear slowly, then vanishes all at once, like the imprint of a hand on glass. Gandalf whimpers as a new image appears: this one is an angry face, its mouth twisted in rage.

'What is it? What's there?' Stig's voice is urgent.

I stare at the stove, my mind racing. The faces appear in dark corners; the movement I saw before was in the deepest shadows. 'Quick, we need more light! I think the darkness makes it easier for them to form.'

Stig rushes to the kitchen and lights several lamps. He returns and hands me one. 'Why can't I see them?'

'I don't know. I can only see them with my left eye. The one that's blind.'

Stig frowns at me, unsure.

I glance into the dark corner of the kitchen and shiver. Yesterday the cabin felt empty without Mormor here. Now it's thick with ghosts. How many faces are waiting to form in the shadows? Thoughts crowd my mind, making me feel dizzy. What do the ghosts want from us . . . ? Can they touch us, or hurt us?

Stig tries the light switch again – nothing – then stares about like a trapped animal. He reaches for the curtain, even though it must be pitch black outside, and tugs it open. A horde of desperate faces stares in. Sad eyes widen in fear; mouths open and close. I scream and Gandalf barks frantically.

Stig drops the curtain. 'What's there?'

I cover my mouth with my hand. So many of them and so pitiful! They must have formed in the condensation, the same as the face in the mirror. I try to speak but the words are like stones in my mouth.

'Martha, please. You're scaring me.'

I push my fear to the pit of my belly. 'Faces – dozens of them. They were piled up on one another, like, like a burial mound. Like in the drawing.'

Stig takes a box of candles from a drawer of the dresser. He hastily lights them and puts them all around the room. Before long, dozens of candles flicker around us. It looks like something from the set of a witchcraft movie.

He stops and catches his breath. 'Are they gone now?'

I look around me, but everything seems normal. 'Yes, I think so.'

A distant howl.

My fingernails dig into my palms.

Stig rushes to the door and checks the bolt, which is still drawn from last night. 'I'll check all the windows are locked!' He dashes from the room and I follow him. Standing between the lounge and bedrooms, I watch as he runs into Mormor's room and rattles the window. He does the same in the spare room and the bathroom.

He darts past me. 'You check the kitchen.'

I step into the lounge, then stop. There's something in the middle of the floor.

The rag doll from the chest.

Its yellow hair is fanned out around its face, making it look even more grotesque than before.

'But how?' I mutter.

I watched Stig run in and out of Mormor's room just now. He didn't have time to go into the chest, even if he could have opened it and taken the doll without me seeing.

I step forward and a smell of mildew and rot fills my nose. When I found the books stacked by themselves, the doll was the only thing left in the chest. That, and Karina's journal. A shiver runs through me. Somebody wants me to find the doll, but why?

Stig opens a kitchen cupboard and grabs a bottle of brandy. I watch as he takes a swig, then wipes his mouth with the back of his hand.

The doll stares at the ceiling with its missing eye. It wears a stained dress, grey with age. The skirt is torn and frayed and one of the sleeves is ripped, exposing a lumpy mottled arm. It doesn't have hands; the arms end in crude stubs. Gandalf sniffs at it suspiciously, then slinks away.

I kneel down and Stig mutters a warning. He drops the bottle of brandy and it rolls under the sofa. I reach out my hand, then sit back on my heels, a bitter taste in my mouth. Surrounded by flickering candles, the doll looks like some kind of sacrificial offering.

Another distant howl.

The image of Yrsa's frozen face flashes into my mind.

Taking a deep breath, I hover my hand over the doll.

'No, Martha! Don't!'

I grasp the *valknut* charm around my neck and it instantly calms me. Without knowing or understanding what I'm doing, I focus my thoughts on the doll, until my consciousness becomes a single dot of intention. At the same time, part of my mind rushes away, expanding . . .

I touch the material and my eyes snap open.

The doll twitches its head. I hold my breath as it rolls over and slumps onto its front, then crawls towards me.

The floor slams into my cheek. Everything goes black.

BLOW OUT THE CANDLES

*D*on't *be afraid of the dark.*

I keep my eyes shut tight, too scared to move or speak.

The voice whispers again. *I know you're afraid, but the darkness is your friend. I am your friend.*

The words are coming from inside my head. Only they're not words; it's a feeling, an impression, which I am putting into words. The voice belongs to me, but the thoughts do not. My brain throbs as I try to make sense of it all.

Who are you?

Karina. I've been trying to make you see me. I've come because you're in danger.

I nod, aware of the absurdity of answering my own thoughts.

You must go to the tree. The Norns will help you put things right.

I can't go out there! Something inside me shrinks with fear. Where is Mormor? Why isn't she speaking to me?

Your grandmother is trapped at the tree, tormented by her regret. She died knowing she had failed to convince your mother to water it, and she feared that no one would.

My stomach wrenches. What do you mean, trapped? Can't you help her?

You are the only one who can save her, Marta. You must go to the tree and get the dead back to the underworld.

But how? I can't! The *draugr* will rip me to shreds, just like Olav and Yrsa!

Go to the tree. Don't fear the Norns.

For a while there is only silence and I wonder if she has gone. When she speaks again, her voice is urgent. *Blow out the candles and keep quiet. Quick!*

Something touches my forehead and my eyes open. The room is on its side, the doll next to me, lifeless.

'Martha? You fainted.' Stig helps me to sit.

'She wants me to blow out the candles.'

'Who?'

'My great-grandmother. She spoke to me through the doll.'

'What? How?' Stig nudges the doll with his foot

and it flips onto its back. Seeing it move again makes me feel queasy, but I don't think Karina meant to scare me.

Mormor warned never to leave a candle burning because it might attract a *draugr*. A gasp escapes me. What have we done? I wanted to stop the faces forming, but we've lit a beacon for the creature – we've drawn it to us!

I turn to Stig. 'Quick, we have to blow out the candles.'

He gives me an exasperated look. 'But you said the darkness helps them to form.'

'I know, but the light attracts the *draugr*!'

The idea of being in the dark with the dead sends a chill through me, but what choice is there? At least I have Stig; I'm not on my own. Whatever's in the cabin hasn't hurt us, but if the *draugr* comes . . . My head sways as I get to my feet.

I take a deep breath and blow out the nearest candle.

Stig's eyes widen in disbelief. I walk around, blowing out more candles. Instantly the shadows become darker. Something rises to my left: the vague outline of shoulders and a head. I turn and gasp as another figure looms up behind me.

Stig catches my arm and spins me around. Fear and confusion flash across his face. 'Martha, don't.'

'Just trust me, Stig. Please.'

Gandalf snarls at the door. Bending down, I hold his head in my hands and peer into his eyes. 'I know you're afraid, but we have to be quiet. We can't make a sound.'

He licks my hand, and for a moment I'm convinced he actually understands. He jumps onto the sofa and curls up, and I pat his head. 'Good boy. I love you, Gandalf.'

I straighten and see Stig standing in the kitchen, surrounded by shadowy figures. My body tenses. For an awful moment he seems like one of them. One of the dead.

Two lamps are flickering on the table. I point at them. 'Please, Stig.'

He shakes his head, refusing to move.

I shut off their flames, plunging us further into darkness. Only one candle remains – on the shelf above the fire. I open the stove door and Stig grabs my shoulder. His jumper brushes me and I get a flash of his fear and powerlessness. Poor Stig can't see what's there; he can't help or protect me. I have to be strong for us both.

I squeeze his hand and he pleads at me with his eyes.

'I know it seems crazy, but I know what I'm doing.'

Stig moves back with a tiny nod. I throw ash over the embers, then take the last candle and step into the middle of the room. The air is icy and thick with shadows. A noise like rushing water fills my ears as shapes manifest in the darkness: a pair of bare feet with no legs; someone's broad shoulders. The sound vibrates faster and a hand materialises in mid-air, just inches from my face. I jump back, terrified it will touch me. Shadows reach out from every side. I struggle to breathe.

'What's happening?' cries Stig.

I look at the wavering flame of the candle in my hand. *Don't fear the darkness, Martha. Don't fear the darkness. Don't fear the* . . .

The flame goes out, extinguished by an unseen force. I drop the candle and blackness devours the room. Stig pulls me onto the sofa and we sit huddled together, his arms around me. I can't stop shivering; it's like the cold is burrowing into my bones.

I hide my face in Stig's hair, then peep out and gasp. The air above our heads glows and pulsates. A group of women stand around us, shielding us in a bubble of light. I recognise Karina's long wavy hair instantly. Next to her is the tiny lady I saw in the photo – Gerd with her feathered cloak, and Trine. I don't know them all, but I know they are the women who went before me. My family.

A dozen voices chant a hushed lullaby. I don't understand what they mean, but the tone of their words is reassuring.

'Ikke vær redd.'

'Familien din er her.'

'Vi er her for å hjelpe.'

'What's happening?' Stig whispers. 'Is there something here, in the room?'

My mouth is too dry to speak. The light from the women starts to fade – I wish I could see his face, but all I can make out is the shape of his head and the glint of his eyes.

Karina taps a finger to her lips.

'Shh,' I whisper to Stig.

Everything is silent. The wind has died to nothing, as if the world no longer exists. Even the darkness holds its breath.

Shuffling outside. Then a low, breathy snort.

Stig's arms tighten around me.

Thump.

The sound of laboured footsteps.

Thump.

It's climbing the steps!

The bubble of light around us shimmers and changes, partly obscuring the room.

The ghostly women are still here, but their faces are blank. They have no features at all.

A single, heavy blow at the door.

I stiffle a sob.

Pots and pans rattle as something slams against the outside of the kitchen wall.

It's moving, fast. Circling us. Trying to find a way in.

Bang. Bang. Bang. Coming from above.

I scream as deafening noise thunders above my head. The banging gets louder and faster, as if the creature is drumming its heels on the roof.

The noise goes on and on. The terrible sound is more than I can bear. I press my hands to my ears. My heart feels like it will explode.

Stig cries out, '*Kjære Gud, få det til å stoppe!*'

And then it stops. Maybe the creature heard him.

Gandalf whines and I lay a hand on him, every

muscle in my body tense. My chest heaves and falls. There's a sound of creaking wood and then the bottom chunk of the door is ripped away. I stare at the silvery moonlight that floods through the gap, the only light in the room.

Suddenly, blackened fingers appear.

I clamp my hand to my mouth and fight a scream. Click. Click. Click.

Curved black claws tap the wood as fingers scrabble at the floor. Scraps of flesh hang from them, the bone white in the moonlight. Stig grabs me tight, as if he sees it too.

The bubble of light around us shimmers and expands. I can no longer see the women, just a swirling vortex of light. The air turns into a transparent metallic liquid that reaches out, filling the room.

The creature's fingers touch it and hold still. Slowly the claws retreat, scraping the floor with a sickening screech.

Please don't come back. Please don't come back. Please don't come back.

I stare at the door, too afraid to move.

My pulse races as I count the seconds. There is no noise. Just the cry of the wind.

'Has it gone?' whispers Stig.

Karina reappears and takes her finger from her lips, then nods.

A shudder runs through me. 'Yes, it's gone.'

A moment later the bubble retracts. The shadows become denser and the women reappear. More faces emerge, all with glowing black eyes. Most are old and wrinkled, but some are about my age. Each one smiles, as if they've been waiting to say hello. The apparitions begin to flicker and fade, like they no longer have the strength to form. I search the crowd, desperately hoping to see Mormor, but she isn't among them. If there was any way she could come back to see me, I know she would.

Karina must be telling the truth: Mormor is trapped at the tree. The thought of going outside makes me feel sick, but I can't leave her out there alone, knowing she needs me. I *have* to help her.

I Don't Want to Die Without Kissing Him

Stig strikes a match, then returns the box to his pocket. The flickering light makes him look older, gaunt almost.

'Is it safe to light a candle?' he whispers.

Gandalf jumps down from the sofa. A moment later, I hear him lapping at his water bowl. He seems at ease, so perhaps the creature is no longer close.

'I think so. Wait, I'll get one.'

I crawl across the floor and reach for a tall pillar candle.

'Quick.' Stig grimaces as the flame touches his fingers.

I hand him the candle and climb back on the sofa. He lights the wick and places it on the floor. Shadows swarm about the room: faces of men, women and children appear and disappear. A little boy wearing striped pyjamas tiptoes a few steps and then vanishes. Seeing them makes me uneasy, but it's not like they want to do us any harm. They don't seem aware of us – or even of each other for that matter.

I wish I could see Mormor. I can't bear to think of her suffering.

Yesterday, when the water went cold and the bathroom lights flickered, I think it was Karina, trying to appear to me. She wouldn't tell me to go out there unless Mormor needed me, and not unless it was safe.

I take a deep breath, my decision made. 'I'm going to the tree.'

Stig's head snaps up. 'What?'

'Karina said Mormor is trapped there, tormented by her regret. I'm the only one who can save her.' I stand up and reach for my boots. 'I have to speak to the Norns. They will tell me what to do.'

'No way! After what just happened?' Stig snatches my arm and tugs me back down. 'You're staying here with me!'

I glare at him. 'I can't leave Mormor out there! The creature has gone now. I can take the torch, and Karina protected me once, she can –'

'No!'

I thump the sofa. 'You would go, if it were your dad!'

Stig's eyes flash with anger. 'That's not fair.'

'But it's the truth! If you thought you could save him, you would try!'

'How do you know for sure Karina can protect you? Maybe she can only keep you safe if you stay in the cabin. Maybe the *draugr* is stronger than she realises. Look what it did to Olav and Yrsa!'

He mutters something in Norwegian and I hang my head and sigh. He's right, I don't know – and there's no safe way to find out.

Stig gazes at the candle on the floor. Eventually he speaks without looking up. 'I really thought we were going to die.'

'I know. So did I. But we didn't.'

'At least wait until the morning. Please.'

I take my phone from my pocket: 6.15 a.m. Another four hours. 'OK,' I sigh. 'I'll go when it gets light.'

Stig challenges me with a stare. 'Wait until your mother arrives. Maybe she can help. You said she was meant to water the tree too.'

I look away, promising nothing. I can't see Mum helping me with this. The old Mum maybe, but since my accident she's been so overprotective, watching me all the time and worrying. No, if anything, she'll fall to pieces and try to stop me doing it.

Silence hangs heavy over the room.

I touch Stig's arm. His jumper is filled with such fear and sadness; I know he wants to cry. 'I'm sorry for what I said about your dad.'

Stig sniffs and says begrudgingly, 'No, you're right. If it was Dad, I would want to help him.' He lifts the candle from the floor and hovers his fingers over the flame, dangerously close. He whispers like a child at a confessional: innocent and sinner, both at the same time. 'I would give anything to see him again.'

He glances at me, his eyes as hard as polished gems, and gives a bitter laugh.

'"Life goes on, Stig." That's what Mum said. The day of the funeral she told me she was going to make a fresh start with Erik. I could stay with them, but not if I carried on like I was, drinking at night and sleeping all day.'

'What did you do?'

He passes his palm over the candle. 'I did what everyone wanted. I went back to school. I helped Nina train and forced myself to smile.' I pull his arm away from the flame and his jumper offers a fleeting memory of Nina. She was completely devoted to Stig, there was never anyone else for her – but for some reason he doesn't like to admit that.

He tucks a strand of hair behind his ear. 'I remember walking home from school one night and looking in at the houses. I stopped at a window and saw a little boy doing a jigsaw puzzle with his father. The house had this orange glow; it was like looking at a Christmas card. I stood there, watching them. They seemed so happy, while I . . . I . . .'

I finish the sentence for him. 'Felt like a house with the windows blown out?'

Stig nods and picks wax from the candle.

'Every night I drank to forget. Every day I woke up wishing I were dead. When I looked in the mirror, it was like looking at a stranger's face, like I was putting eyeliner on another person. But as long as I acted OK, people were happy.'

A shadowy girl about my age with short dark hair stands by the door. She wears a simple shift dress and has bare feet. She doesn't seem like the others, just passing through. She glares at me accusingly, and I shift in my seat, feeling uncomfortable.

Stig sniffs and I turn my attention back to him. 'I know how it feels to see a stranger in the mirror. After the accident everyone wanted me to be the Martha I was before, but I couldn't.'

'What happened?'

'Nothing. I just hid in my room.'

Stig sighs. 'I wish I was like you.'

A huff of disbelief escapes me. 'Why?'

His breath is so soft the candle barely flickers. 'Because at least you were honest. I'm always lying and pretending to be something I'm not. I've been doing it so long I can't stop. It's like I've forgotten how to be myself, and I hate it.'

I sit back in my seat, surprised by the anger in his voice.

We say nothing for a while, and for some reason my thoughts turn to the day they removed my bandages in hospital. I cried with joy when I saw Mum's face, but she wasn't smiling. A nurse put a mirror in my hand and I saw why. The left side of my head was bruised and swollen, the flesh a nasty shade of blue and yellow, like some kind of mouldy, squashed fruit. My left eye was cloudy white and stared upward in a

166

weird direction, as if transfixed by something only it could see. A gash on my left cheek held together with black stitches completed my new look.

Mum cried whenever she could bring herself to look at me. No matter how often she asked me how I was feeling, I knew I mustn't make things any harder for her. I couldn't hide my face, but I could at least hide my feelings. I could at least pretend to be OK.

I glance at Stig. 'I don't know about that. We all lie sometimes, especially if it's to protect the people we care about. Anyway, you're not pretending with me now, are you?'

Stig smiles and the crease in his bottom lip deepens. 'No, I feel different when I'm with you.'

My heart pirouettes and does a tiny somersault. 'Different how?'

'Well, yesterday when I woke up I didn't want to die. I wanted to make you pancakes.'

I laugh softly. 'They *were* pretty good pancakes.'

Stig grins. 'I'm glad I was here to make them for you.'

He licks his lips and I realise I've been gazing at his mouth. Our heads are so close they're almost touching.

'Martha, do you think some things are meant to be?'

'Maybe.'

He looks at me intently. 'It has to mean something, us finding each other, doesn't it?'

I try to think of something to say, but I can't. A movement at the corner of my eye makes me glance at the door. The shadows there are empty, but I can sense the girl still in the room. I can feel her drawing closer, listening.

Stig picks wax from his fingers. 'I don't know if I believe in God, but I have thought a lot about fate. If I hadn't phoned Dad that night, he would still be alive. Or do you think it was his time?'

I sigh, wishing I had the answers. Although I can't know for sure, instinct tells me that the pattern of our lives is laid down before we are even born. I think back to something Mormor told me once. We were in the shed, setting up her old loom. She pointed to the vertical lines of yarn fixed to the wooden frame. 'There are circumstances in our life that cannot be changed: when and where we are born, who our parents are.' She tugged hard at the yarn. 'This is the warp. It's fixed, see?' I nodded, and she placed my hand on the lines running across the frame from side to side. 'This is the weft – the yarn that goes over and under the warp. This part we can change.' I looked at her, confused, and she hugged me close. 'A person who has a poor start in life can still weave a good tapestry, if they make the right choices.' She whispered, 'Strengthen what's there, my child, and no one will notice the holes.'

I hadn't thought about it properly before, but now I realise she was talking about fate. Half of who we are is given to us and can't be changed, but the rest depends on our actions. Something tells me Stig had nothing to do with his dad's death – he died because of the choices he made.

'It was just his time,' I say, even though I don't really believe that. It wasn't fate that made his dad crash his car, but if the idea offers Stig some comfort . . .

He glances at me hopefully. There is pain and longing in his eyes, as if he desperately wants to believe me. He drops his gaze and picks at the candle, and I rest my hand on his arm. Something deep inside the material assures me I am right. It's not the usual fleeting image or feeling I get; it's like a truth dyed into the fibres of the wool that's always been there but I've never noticed before.

I open my mouth and a cage of conviction closes around my heart, the truth inescapable inside. The Norns may have cut the cord, but his dad died because he'd been drinking. It was nothing to do with Stig. 'I know you feel guilty, but it wasn't your fault.'

Stig bites his lip and looks away.

I squeeze his arm and then tug at his jumper. 'I can feel it, *here*.'

Stig lets out a shaky breath as if he finally believes me. 'I'm glad I met you,' he whispers. He shifts forward on the sofa and lowers his face towards me, and I can smell the alcohol on his breath. My pulse quickens as I close my eyes, waiting for his lips to touch mine. Instead he kisses the top of my head.

He rests back on the sofa, seemingly exhausted, while I sit in a daze, waiting for a moment that doesn't come. I was sure he was going to kiss me. You kiss a child on the head; is that how he sees me? I don't understand. We seem to connect in every way. My thoughts

169

become hard-edged. It's because of my face. It has to be.

'I'm going to the bathroom,' I mutter.

I stand and light an oil lamp, then carry it to the bathroom and place it on the sink. After I use the toilet, I wash my hands and splash freezing water on my face. The flickering light of the lamp makes me look different, harsher somehow – but not different enough.

I cover the left side of my face with my hand. The mirror shows a girl with high cheekbones and a small nose covered with freckles. Her eye is green-blue like the sea, her eyebrow and eyelashes so pale they're almost white. Her lips are small but perfectly formed. I raise the corners of my mouth and a pretty girl smiles back.

And then I take my hand away.

The pretty girl is replaced by a monster. Its eyeball is permanently rotated in the socket, so that it stares upward to the left, making it seem deranged. The lid droops slightly and the whole eye is milky white, clouding the black of the pupil. A jagged scar runs from above the eyebrow to an inch below the eye, like someone attacked it with a knife.

Resentment curls my fingers into a fist.

Dad arranged for a private surgeon to see me at the hospital in Oslo. He was meant to replace my eye with a false one. I would still be blind on that side, but at least the eye could be fixed to look straight ahead. The surgeon took scans of my brain, but the news wasn't good. 'No one will operate, at least not yet, I'm afraid. The risk of further damage is too great.' My hopes splintered under the weight of his words.

I lean in towards the mirror and stare at my good eye. *Stupid, stupid, stupid. When will you learn? Don't hope and no one can hurt you: not the doctors, not Stig. Not anyone.*

When I go back to the lounge, Stig is snoring softly. I gaze at him while he sleeps, my heart full of longing. I know it's silly, but I don't want to die without kissing him. If the *draugr* comes back, I want to feel that I have lived. That I've had a perfect moment with someone I really care about. Someone who cares about *me*.

The shadowy dead flit about the room and I catch a glimpse of the girl. Her eyes are as hard as flint. She seems familiar, as if I've seen her face somewhere. The journals maybe . . .

I sit on the sofa and brush my hand over Stig's jumper, but it only speaks of his dad. I thump a cushion, then rest my head on it. As soon as I close my eyes, sleep wraps its arms around me – pulling me head first into a nightmare.

No One Should Suffer This Fate

A figure stands by the well: a woman in a cloak, her shoulders hunched with age and her face shaded by a hood. A flurry of snow drifts down but not a single flake settles on her. There is something eerie about the stillness, as if she's always been here in the gloom, waiting.

Her voice is harsh and cracked. 'Come.'

Something tugs at me, deep inside, and I stare at my boots as my feet move of their own accord. I shuffle through the snow, my legs trembling, then stop before her.

'Closer,' she rasps.

I take another step forward. I'm close enough to touch her cloak if I dared. I raise my eyes and see the wizened face of an old lady. Her skin is wrinkled and her cheeks are sunken red.

She dips her gnarled hand in the well. 'Look deeply.'

I peer into inky blackness. Pinpoints of light flicker in the water as a constellation of stars explodes under her fingertips. Shapes swirl up from the depths. The ripples subside and a face looms under the water: the doctor from the hospital. The image changes and I see myself bumping into a woman at the airport. The water darkens, and a face as white and smooth as a pebble floats to the surface: Brian from the plane. Questions bubble in my mind, so many I don't know which to ask first.

The old woman glances over her shoulder, and when she turns back to me, two other women step out from her shadow. I stumble away and nearly fall to the ground. The first wears her hood down, revealing a beautiful heart-shaped face and long black hair. She has the same high cheekbones and pointed chin as the old lady, and the same fierce dark eyes. The second seems younger, a girl around my age, her face partly obscured by her hood. They look like the three women carved into the chest: the Norns.

I clutch my head. How long have the Norns been watching me? I would never have lost my footing and fallen from the tree if I hadn't seen that face in the bark. Confusion hardens to anger. 'You made me fall, didn't you?'

They fix me with a sharp gaze. 'This is the destiny you chose before birth, but there is always another path.'

My fists clench. I point at my blind eye. 'I didn't *choose* this!'

The girl grips my wrist and her fingers burn like ice. 'Because your mother did not water the tree, the dead escaped. It is now *your* destiny to return them. To do that, you must be able to see them – and such power calls for sacrifice.'

I glare at her and she yanks me towards the well. 'Odin gouged out his eye for one sip of wisdom. He hanged himself until nearly dead in order to discover the runes!' She dips a hand in the water and I see my reflection – only it's not me. Both my eyes and mouth are sewn shut. 'This is what will happen if you don't see clearly.'

I cry out and pull free from her grasp.

The beautiful Norn touches my shoulder. 'You have much to learn. Come.'

I stand outside the circle as the Norns take each other's hands and begin to chant. The sound is like nothing I've heard before. At first a sighed whisper, wind stirring the treetops, and then growing and becoming louder, like the thrum of rain on a roof. The chant ebbs and flows, the voices merging to weave a pattern of sound.

As they sing, silver threads leap from their mouths, forming delicate shapes in the air. The chant continues to build – at once beautiful, strange, and haunting – until the strands become ropes. Letting go of one another's hands, the Norns grab hold of the cords, passing them between themselves again and again, under and over, weaving a shimmering cloth of light. Flashes of silver shoot into the sky, making the surface of the well glimmer.

The chant ends and they turn to face me, holding the cloth between them. Each tiny thread moves and pulsates with light. The girl gestures for me to touch it. I pause, unsure, and then grasp it. A million voices cry out: men, women and children from across time and from all nations – telling me their fears, joys and sorrows.

A rush of emotion electrifies me, surging along my arm and body until my scalp tingles. The threads – they're souls!

Sparks ignite in my chest. Every nerve ending burns as my mind races and expands. I'm spinning through clouds, flying over forests and mountains, oceans, deserts and cities. Billions of voices speak as images flash before my eyes: blood pulsating through an umbilical cord; a mud hut and a pregnant woman; a guttural scream and the cry of a newborn. The faces of the Norns, weaving energy with their song and pulling the baby's cry into the tapestry of creation.

Then the hut is gone and I'm in the sky. Below me is a busy city street with hordes of people rushing in every direction. Shimmering silver light spirals around each person, yet at the same time they're connected in a huge, intricate web of energy.

Understanding explodes in my head. I feel as if I've climbed the highest mountain and I'm looking down on all creation. I want to laugh and cry and sing with joy.

The girl raises her arm and metal glints in the half-light. I gasp as she brings her shears down on the cloth. They close with a cruel crunch, sending scraps of material spiralling like burnt ash from a bonfire. I fall to my knees with them, my heart cut in two.

All those lives lost – ended with a single cut of her shears. The old man in Delhi who died in his sleep, surrounded by his family; the teenager in Zambia shot down by soldiers; the mother in Ireland who cuddled her children as she died in a hospital bed. I feel each and every death.

I crawl towards a piece of fabric no bigger than a child's coat. I want to gather them up and keep them safe. I want to stitch them back together. Kneeling in the snow, I stare at the darkening sky as thousands of scraps swirl and catch on the branches above me. How can such a beautiful shimmering cloth be reduced to this – to blackened scraps?

And then I see Mormor, desperately trying to catch a piece of material from the tree.

'Mormor, it's me, Martha!'

My heart aches. I get to my feet and rush to her.

She jumps and snatches for the cloth, even though it's hopelessly out of her reach. 'Please, Mormor!' I reach out but my hand glides straight through her. She turns and her eyes are empty black orbs.

My chest hurts so much I can barely breathe. Each branch of the tree is covered with scraps of material. They sway in the breeze; a million tiny corpses.

Suddenly there are hordes of people around Mormor, all of them grasping.

I turn on the Norns. 'Why have you done this?'

Three voices speak as one. 'These are the ones who died consumed by regret.'

I look at the pitiful figures. No one should suffer this fate.

'Why can't the dead rest in peace?'

The beautiful Norn looks at me, an ocean of kindness in her eyes. 'The dead should rest with Hel until it is time for them to reincarnate, but no one tended to the tree and now it is rotting. Most of the souls that escaped were drawn to their regrets, hanging on the branches. Some will be trapped here for eternity unless you help them. Your ancestors left the underworld in search of you – they risked being lost forever, because only you can put things right.'

'Me? But you're the ones who control fate!'

The young girl steps forward. Her voice is as sharp as her shears. 'The future is bound by the past. Some things cannot be changed.'

I turn back to the beautiful Norn, but she shakes her head. 'Skuld is right. Besides, we have no power over the dead, and Hel cannot leave her realm.'

I start to ask another question, but I'm stopped by the strangeness of what I see. The three figures step together to become one. There is one cloak, one hooded face: each countenance transposed on the other two. A single woman walks to the tree and lays her palm against its trunk.

'Wait! How do I save Mormor?'

Rough bark creeps over her hand like a scaly rash, turning her fingernails to wood. Her hand and arm disappear into the trunk, followed by her leg and torso. The wind groans as she steps into the tree and vanishes, leaving only a chill on the air.

I press my ear to the bark and a raspy voice echoes in my head, 'Come to the tree.'

PURE EVIL STARES AT ME

I wake confused, caught between sorrow and panic. The dream releases its grip on me and I glance at the window. We made it through the night at least – the creature didn't come back. Judging from the light creeping under the curtain, it has to be at least eleven o' clock. And then I remember, and my heart sinks.

I sit up and rub my neck. Stig is in the kitchen with his back to me, making coffee. The sleeves of his sloppy, oversized jumper are rolled up, showing his strong forearms. Something inside me flickers at the sight of his tight jeans and long hair. I want to put my arms around him and hold him tight. I pull my gaze away, reminding myself of how rejected I felt last night.

I step into the kitchen and he hands me a cup of coffee. I take it with a small 'thanks', then reach past him and open the curtain. Huge white flakes swirl down, as fat as goose feathers. The tree is only just visible through the snow. Its branches are still, as if it's gathering strength.

I swallow a mouthful of coffee. 'About last –'

Stig speaks at the same time. 'I've been –'

We look at one another awkwardly. I wrap my fingers around my cup. 'You first.'

'I wanted to thank you for what you said about Dad, about it not being my fault.'

An image of the Norn with her shears flashes into my mind. I consider telling Stig about my dream, but then I remember the kiss that didn't come and how stupid I felt.

'That's OK,' I say, forcing myself to smile.

He glances at my face as if he expects me to say something. I finish my coffee and then lay the cup by the sink.

Stig's eyes widen as I reach for my coat and shrug into it. 'You're not going out there?'

I grit my teeth and wait for the argument to come.

'Wait a few hours. If your mum isn't here before it gets dark, then –'

'And if her plane can't land, or the ferry isn't running? Or her car gets stuck in the snow?'

Stig glares at me and I return his stare. 'I promised to wait until it got light, and I have. But I can't put if off any more. Mormor is out there – she needs me!'

Stig grabs the back of a chair and it screeches against the floor. 'I won't let you go out there, even if I have to tie you to this chair!'

My chest flushes with anger. 'Don't be so ridiculous!'

I stomp towards the door, but he blocks my way with the chair and I fall over it, cursing.

'Please, it's not safe for you. I *can't* let you go!'

I push myself up, my cheeks hot with embarrassment. 'Because I'm half blind? I can manage, thanks.'

'You're not seeing things clearly!' he yells.

I point to my left eye. 'I wonder why?'

Stig huffs and flaps his arms. 'All the comments you keep making about your eye. Don't think I haven't noticed! I don't know why you have to make such a big deal of it.'

I step back, hurt and shocked. 'What?'

'Yes, your left eye looks weird and you have a scar, but it's not that interesting!'

I open my mouth then close it again, too upset to answer. I had hoped that because of the goth thing he might like girls who are extreme-looking. He might like me *because* I look different.

His voice softens. 'Actually, your eye is the *least* interesting thing about you.'

I pause, feeling deflated, but also wondering if there might be a compliment in there somewhere. Stig takes advantage of my hesitation and pushes past me. He stands by the front door, barring my way.

'What were you going to say to me just now?' he asks.

'Nothing.'

He folds his arms across his chest.

I shove on my boots, then grab my hat and scarf, not looking at him. 'It can wait.'

He gently touches the collar of my coat. 'Please don't go. Your mum will be here soon. It's safer inside.'

I sigh, unable to meet his gaze. I felt so close to him last night. So close I was sure he was going to kiss me. I think about the hordes of people snatching at the tree, all haunted by regret, tormented by the things they wish they'd done differently. I can't face the thought of him rejecting me again, but if I don't tell him how I feel, will I always regret it? It was so easy for Skuld to chop away a life with her shears – if the creature is out there, maybe it will be my thread she cuts next.

Stig strokes my cheek and I put my hand over his, meaning to pull it away. As soon as I touch his skin, my chest tightens. I don't want to spend my life hiding away, not getting close. Afraid to be hurt.

Stig swallows hard. 'I couldn't bear it if –'

I stand on tiptoes and kiss him, full on the lips.

He pulls away like he's been slapped.

Anger and shame burn inside me.

'Martha?'

'I'm sorry! I didn't mean to . . .' I splutter. 'It won't happen again, OK!'

Dizzy with hurt, I push past him and reach for the door.

'I like you, Martha. I do! It's just –'

'You don't have to explain!'

Keeping my head down, I slide back the bolt and yank the door open. Wind and snow roar into the cabin. I know what he's going to say. He likes me, but not in that way.

Stig grabs my arm. 'Wait! Don't go like this.'

Why can't he leave me alone? Haven't I been humiliated enough?

I shrug him off and stumble into a blizzard. A tear spills from my eye as I jump down the porch steps, my boots sinking in snow. I raise my arm against the vicious spit of ice and gasp as the cold air burns my throat. Anger pumps my legs faster. I trudge around the side of the cabin, tears streaming down my frozen cheeks.

I pull my gloves from my pockets, but my hands are shaking and I can't get them on. 'Stupid idiot!' I should have put them on before I came out. The snow is coming down so heavily I can only just see the tree. I shove my bare hands into my armpits and lumber towards it.

'*Faen! Faen! Faen!*'

Stig's voice gets louder with each curse. I wipe my face on my sleeve as a black shape half runs, half stumbles towards me. He's wearing his coat but hasn't stopped to put on his hat. The snow is whirling thick and fast. I blink and see him, only to lose him again.

'I wanted to kiss you! I've never met anyone like you!'

I turn towards his voice. 'So why didn't you then?'

A cruel wind cuts into my face. My pulse races as I stare about me. Suddenly there is only white. No cabin, no tree, no up or down.

'Stig?'

The snow is blinding. Gandalf barks in warning, but I can't see him. I'm somewhere between the tree and the cabin, but I don't know which is closer. I take a few steps, then stumble. My breath is hard and fast, leaving great plumes on the air.

'Martha!'

My name comes to me over the wind, and I whip around. Not trusting my sight, I stagger towards Stig's voice. I see the back of his head and my heart falters. He's a dozen paces away to my left, walking in the wrong direction.

I run towards him. 'Stig!'

He spins around.

A dark shape emerges from the snow. A half-human creature.

I gasp as it strides towards me. Strips of brown leathery skin hang from its skull, and its head is covered with dirty, matted hair.

I stand, unable to move, the air frozen in my lungs.

Stig runs towards me from the other side, waving his arms and yelling.

It's coming right at me.

Stig yanks my arm, jolting me out of my trance. 'Go, Martha!' He pushes me away, then turns to face the creature. I run, desperately hoping I'm heading for the cabin.

Gasping for breath, I look back for Stig, but he's not there. He's on the ground.

'No!'

I stare at the thing crouched over Stig's body. It lifts its head and yellow eyes bulge in its face; its mouth a swollen, red wound.

My mind splinters into a million pieces. I rush towards Stig, then stop. Maybe he's just injured . . . Maybe . . . Maybe . . .

Stig's arm is bent awkwardly beneath him. I watch as his chest heaves and falls.

Please, Stig, get up. Just get up. I will him to stand and run. But he doesn't.

Red seeps into the snow, too much red.

Stig's eyes stare at the sky. His chest stops moving.

I scream until there's nothing left.

The creature twists its head and pure evil stares at me.

BLACK HOLE OF MY NIGHTMARES

The *draugr* stands to its full terrifying height. Scraps of leather hang from its emaciated body; a bit of material flaps in the wind, caught on a jagged bone that juts through the rotting skin of its chest. Yellow eyes stare at me through a curtain of snow.

Stig lies at the creature's feet, his face tinged blue. Snowflakes settle on his hair and melt into the blood that gushes from the wound in his neck. I watch transfixed as a river of red seeps out of him. Steam rises from his blood, yet he looks so cold.

The *draugr* steps towards me and the stench of decay turns my stomach.

Run. I need to run.

My heart races, but I can't move.

A flash of movement makes me turn my head: a familiar shape bounds through the blizzard. 'Gandalf!' He jumps in front of me, hackles raised, lips pulled back to reveal sharp, dangerous teeth. He snaps and snarls with the ferocity of an animal willing to fight to the death.

The *draugr* strides towards me. Its filthy hair streams in the wind and blood drips from the claws of its hand, leaving a trail of red in the snow.

Gandalf's barks become frenzied. Steam rises from his body and foam drips from his jaws. He dips his front legs, ready to attack, then leaps into the air and sinks his teeth into the creature's arm. The *draugr* stumbles, unbalanced, and swings its arm, lifting the dog high off the ground. Gandalf's jaw is locked, refusing to let go.

The *draugr* punches the dog with its other hand and I wince at the brutal blow. 'Leave him alone!' I scream. I run towards Gandalf, determined to save him. The *draugr* throws open its arm and the dog flies through the air and thumps to the ground. He gives a pitiful whimper and is silent. Tears stream down my face. 'I'm sorry, Gandalf! I'm sorry!'

Sobbing, I lurch away, arms flailing desperately. The dark shape of the tree shivers ahead, only a dozen paces from me. The Norns – they have to help!

Something tugs at my boot and I fall head first in the snow. Cursing, I roll onto my back and pull my foot free from a root. Branches sway above me, dark arms warning of danger too late. The tree is so close. If I can just . . .

The *draugr* stands over me and its putrid smell makes me want to heave. Its left cheek has rotted away, leaving a flap of skin. The muscles around its mouth tighten into a parody of a smile.

I crawl backwards and try to scream, but my voice is a strangled sob.

My ancestors saved me before; maybe they can again. 'Karina! Help me, please!'

The *draugr* stares at me with lifeless eyes.

I get to my feet and command myself to breathe. Holding the *valknut* charm, I try to remember how I felt when I touched the doll. I dredge up all the power I have in me, through my legs and into my stomach and chest.

A savage voice that's not my own rages from inside me. 'Up, you dead! Rise up and save me!'

The sky darkens and the wind screams.

A shape appears on my left. The shimmering outline of a woman: Karina! Her face is set with determination. She charges at the *draugr* and it swings its arm, making the apparition explode into snow.

I raise my arm and shield my eyes as another figure rises up. A tiny old woman with long, flowing hair. Gerd runs at the creature and it turns and swings, smashing her likeness to smithereens.

Another snowy woman rises, and another. The *draugr* destroys one of my ancestors, only for another to appear. It grunts as it punches its way through them. They're slowing it down, but it's not enough.

I race to the tree and hammer on its trunk. I need

the Norns to tell me how to save Mormor and get her back to the underworld. But not Stig! He's so young – he can't die! The Norns have to change this.

A familiar chiselled face appears in the bark and my shout dies in my throat. A leg emerges, followed by a shoulder, until finally the old woman stands before me. Her face is calm and untroubled. Two figures step out from her shadow: the beautiful Norn with her hair flowing in the wind, and the girl, her face partly hidden by her hood.

Something glints from the folds of Skuld's cloak. It's she who cuts the cords, she who decides when a life ends. I point at her shears and yell, 'You killed Stig! You did this!'

The girl looks at a scrap of fabric fluttering on a nearby branch and holds out her arm. The cloth whips through the air and flies into her hand. She holds it out to me but I refuse to take it. Stig can't be dead. He can't!

She looks at me with cold eyes. 'Don't you want to know?'

I gaze at the pitiful rag. I want to know everything there is to know about him, but not like this. I want the living, breathing Stig. I want to feel the warmth of his arms around me. I want us to share our secrets in front of the fire.

She uncurls a finger as if to release the cloth.
'No!'

I snatch it from her and clutch it to my chest. The material speaks only of sorrow: every regret of Stig's life distilled into a single bitter drop. Remorse writhes under my fingertips; strands of self-accusation twist and turn, tying themselves into a knot of grief. Stig's guilt for calling his father that night. He should never have walked out on his mum. Shame, guilt, self-loathing. The cloth races through each misgiving of his life.

It starts to show me Nina but I pull away, not wanting to see. And then it shows the two of us together and I can barely breathe. Stig regretted not kissing me.

The cloth shows me an image of myself laughing and playing in the snow. I see myself as Stig saw me, and a rush of warmth spreads through my chest. My face is disfigured – it's not like he didn't notice – but Stig saw beauty in me too.

I feel the yearning he felt – he wanted to kiss me, but he was afraid he wasn't good enough for me. Worried that he was too damaged inside to make anyone happy.

I glance up to see the *draugr* battling the dead, fighting its way towards me.

The material tugs at my mind and a different thread of memory catches. I see myself shivering on the sofa. Stig is pulling off my boots. He wanted to tell me how he felt, but the time wasn't right; I was too upset. And then I see him kissing me on the head. He wanted me so much, but he was overwhelmed by emotion. He had finally started to accept he wasn't responsible for his dad's death – but his blame and anger had been holding him together. Letting go of them made him feel vulnerable, and he needed space to process his feelings. How could I have been so selfish?

The *draugr* is getting close. I need to run but the cloth won't let me. Another memory demands to be seen: me standing at the front door, determined to leave the cabin. Stig gazes into my eyes. The strength of his emotion makes my heart beat fast. He felt so at home with me; he felt he could be himself and tell me anything. He was fascinated by my gift, by everything about me. He couldn't bear the idea of losing me. When I kissed him, he pulled away because it felt as if I was kissing him goodbye.

And now it's too late.

I wipe my eyes and see the *draugr* nearly upon me.

Clenching my fists, I turn on the Norns. 'You control fate. You can change this!'

The old woman ignores me and walks towards the tree.

'Please! There has to be something you can do!'

The Norns step close together, ready to merge back into one. Dread creeps through me. The *draugr* is moments away. They're going to leave me to die.

I grab the charm around my neck, then take a deep breath and find the power inside me. My words are a savage, primal scream, 'I am a daughter of Odin! I command you to help me!' I stamp on a root and the ground trembles as branches shudder above. If it would bring Stig back, I would take an axe to the trunk. I would set it on fire and watch it burn.

The youngest Norn regards me coolly, a trace of admiration in her gaze. 'Only Hel, Queen of the Underworld, can give back a life.'

'Then take me to Hel!'

The beautiful Norn tilts her head. 'Few have made the journey, and fewer still have returned. You understand what you are asking?'

I nod, afraid but determined not to show it. The two other Norns step into her shadow and they become one.

'Very well.' She grabs my wrist and ice shoots into my veins. I stare at my arm as the coldness creeps into me. I try to pull away, but I can't. I drop to my knees, and a tree root slithers over my calf and tightens around my thigh. I watch it like it's happening to someone else. Twisting my body, I try to sit up, strain to pull free. The root drags me across the snowy ground and I wince as the back of my head bumps and grazes over gnarled roots.

And then I'm lying among rotting leaves in the dank, stinking chamber of the tree. I've been here before, in another dream. I need to wake up. I need to wake . . .

Dirt patters onto my face and into my mouth. Earth covers my eyes. I spit out soil and scream, but it's too late. I'm being swallowed into the black hole of my nightmares.

WHERE THERE IS THREAD, THERE IS A BLADE

My hands grasp empty air as I fall into darkness. Roots prod at my stomach, yank at my hair. They scratch at my face and tear at my clothes. Forcing me down, swallowing me whole. Above me, gnarled arms twist and turn, until the world becomes a tiny circle of light.

Thud.

I land heavily and pain shoots through my hands and knees. Panting hard, I reach out to feel a wall of compressed soil. I grope in front of me, to the sides, behind, then look upwards. The walls are smooth: no roots to haul myself up, no foothold to climb.

I stand and search for some weakness in the earth: a door, a tunnel, something. There's barely enough room to lie down; I can't stay in here! There has to be a way out, has to be. But there isn't. With dirt-thick fingers I smear away a tear. I thought I would give anything for Stig to live, but I can't stay trapped in this dark hole.

Long minutes pass. I stamp my feet to try and stay warm. Someone will come soon, something will happen. My breath hangs on the air as the cold gnaws at my thoughts. Maybe I've been left here to die.

I scream so hard my throat hurts.

The light dims and I look up and see the silhouette of a head and shoulders. At last! Someone must have heard me. Maybe it's Mum. I wave my arms. 'Hey, I'm down here! Please hel—'

Clawed fingers curl over the edge of the hole and a fresh wave of panic hits me.

Scrabbling sounds. Soil rains down, covering my hair and face.

The *draugr* – it's trying to get in!

I stumble back and fall to the ground. The creature grunts and bellows, and I bury my face in my hands, my stomach roiling at its smell. More soil patters down on me, on and on, until my hair is thick with dirt.

An enraged howl, and then everything stops. The only sound is the thud of my heart.

I blink and shield my eyes against a shaft of brilliant sunlight. Perhaps the light made it go away? Weak with relief, I drop onto my side and curl into a ball. The sun's warmth is only faint, but it's wonderful to feel it on my skin. I rock myself gently for the longest time. I yearn to sleep, to escape, but I keep my eyes open, afraid to close them in case I never wake.

I don't know how long I lie there, staring at the earth. Overcome with tiredness, my eyes eventually close. The sound of my own ragged breathing fills my ears, and then my breath slows and I am slipping away, spinning into darkness, speeding through a tunnel, twisting and . . .

I jolt awake.

Someone is stroking my hair, just like Mum did when I woke up in hospital. A cold, bony finger traces the scar on my cheek. It doesn't feel . . . I swallow hard, afraid to even think the words.

Something shifts beside me, a cold looming presence.

Every muscle in my body freezes. I don't dare breathe.

A strange low voice. 'You do not belong here.'

Whatever is whispering, it isn't human.

A hand tugs my shoulder.

I turn and see a huge figure and gasp in fright. Twice the size of a normal human being, it sits hunched over me, wearing a tattered robe, its face shadowed by a hood. It looks just like the drawing in the journal: the dark mother, Hel. She stands up, impossibly tall in the tiny space, and a flutter of wings fills the air. I cough and blink against the dust as a cloud of moths flies out from her cloak and spirals up through the tunnel. Hel throws back her hood. The right side of her face is beautiful, with flawless white skin and long black hair. The left side is a bald skull. I recoil and twist my head away.

Hel squats, so that my face is level with her waist. Coldness emanates from her, and I shiver as she leans close. As she peers at me, I see her hair is crawling with bugs.

She lifts my chin with a skeletal finger and I look at the living part of her face. Her eye holds an ocean of emotion, as if every drop of human sorrow has washed upon her shores. Afraid to look into the empty socket of her other eye, I stare at the ground.

Hel rests a heavy, living hand on my shoulder. 'You are weary, I know, but it is not your time. Why are you here?'

Sadness wells inside me as I search for words big enough to hold my pain, words I can pour my sorrow into: the ache of losing Mormor, my anger that Stig is dead. But no words come, only a memory: Stig and I staring at each other before I marched stubbornly off into the snow. There were so many things we wanted to say, but our feelings were new and fragile – a fledgling thing. Like a bird pushed from the nest before it had a chance to fly, my hopes lie bloodied and battered. How can I tell Hel that I want what was never mine? I want back what I almost had. I want the chance to be loved. I want . . .

Hel wipes a tear from my cheek, and my words rush out. 'Stig thought I was beautiful, he really cared. I've only just met him. Please, I can't lose him!' I glance at the living side of her face, hoping to find some tenderness that suggests she'll let him live, but the horror of her skeletal teeth and jaw is too strong and I look away.

'Please can I see him?'

'Stig is not here.'

Dismay tugs at the deepest part of me. 'Then where is he?'

'His spirit still resides in his body. I have not called him to me yet.'

'Does that mean –'

Her voice is hard-edged. 'It means what I said.'

I study my boots, not daring to meet her gaze. 'And Mormor?'

Hel stands and stares down at me. 'She should be here, but she is trapped in the world of the living, tormented by her regrets, along with all the other restless dead.'

Guilt wraps around my heart. Mormor is out there. She needs me. I should be helping her. Somehow I have to make all of this right.

'Please, will you hel—'

Hel strides away, the space around her expanding with each step she takes. At first there is only a subtle change in light, as if my sight is adjusting to the dark, and then the image changes and she's seated on a throne and I am standing before her.

'Look at me,' she commands.

I swallow hard and try to focus just on the beautiful part of her face, but the deathly side is too awful and I turn away.

'Look at me,' she repeats.

This time I let my gaze rest on all of her. I look into her living eye, and see my own face reflected there. Like her, I am made up of two sides, half of me damaged and scarred. I stare into her empty eye socket and see myself reflected there too. Self-pity, insecurity, self-loathing, they bubble up inside me like tar. All the things I don't want to feel. The person I don't want to be. A sob catches in my throat as I see myself laid bare.

A caw of a raven breaks the spell. It flies over my head, then lands on top of Hel's throne and puffs out its grey-feathered chest. Another raven, smaller than the first, flaps down to stand on the opposite side.

'Muninn here is fond of stories, aren't you now?' Hel raises her right arm and the smaller of the two birds hops onto her hand. 'Would you care to tell Marta here how I came to be Queen of the Underworld?'

The raven dips its body and, to my amazement, a rich, sonorous voice replies, 'No, mistress, for it is your story to tell.'

He flutters back to his perch, and Hel turns to me. 'No one can tell the story of you, but you. Some people are gifted with a gilded tongue. They will tell you who you are with such conviction that you may actually believe them, but this is a reflection, not the truth, for the story of you is not yet written.'

She leans back. 'You will find these voices in your head also. You will tell yourself how you are a poor victim. Pay no heed and instead look to your soul, for that is where you originate. You write the story of you every day with your thoughts, words and deeds. You *create* yourself. You get to decide your story. No one else. You.'

A tiny flame of understanding catches inside me.

The edges of the room turn dark, and suddenly Hel is standing before a roaring hearth. The human side of her face is beautiful in the firelight but the deathly side is full of shadows; they flicker in her hollow eye socket and curl around her empty jaw. She stares into the flames as she speaks: 'The gods found me so loathsome to look upon, they cast me down here.'

'But I thought . . . So who made you queen?'

My eyes jolt open and I'm back in the hole, my knees to my chest. Alone. I was dreaming or having some kind of vision . . . Something crawls over my leg and I flick away a beetle. The ground is writhing with insects. Panting hard, I grip my *valknut* charm to stop my panic. I have to get back there.

Drumming pounds in my ears. I listen to the steady beat, close my eyes and let myself be taken.

This time I see Hel wearing a glorious gown of shining dark feathers, a gleaming black crown on her head. At last I understand: Hel wrote her *own* story.

'No one made you queen. You made yourself queen.'

She smiles and pulls an axe from the folds of her cloak. 'To kill the *draugr*, you must sever its head from its body with a single, clean blow.'

I crane my neck upward, my legs weak beneath me. How am I meant to kill that thing? Everyone who's taken a stand against it has died – it killed Yrsa and Olav, and they had a gun. I only escaped before because my ancestors protected me.

Hel holds the axe out to me, and a deep sound – 'Nau-dizzz' – reverberates in my head as a rune symbol draws itself onto the blade: a vertical line, crossed by a diagonal one. Hel runs the edge of the weapon across her fleshy palm, and I wince at the ooze of red. She makes a fist above the blade, and blood drips onto the markings. The symbol absorbs the blood and glows white, pulsating with energy. I want to ask what the rune means, but I push the question away, afraid to ask in case I wake to find myself back in the hole.

Hel notices me staring at the axe and smiles knowingly. 'Day and night, life and death, joy and pain . . . there cannot be one without the other. Where there is thread, there is a blade. The knife cuts the umbilical cord; without it there is no life. At the end, the Norn's shears cut the silver cord.'

She removes a rope from her waist. 'With this you can save your grandmother and the rest of the dead.' She wraps the rope around my middle and raw elemental energy surges through me, making my body tremble. I gasp as the cord tightens itself around my waist and slithers into my coat pocket. 'Place one end in the hole of the tree and hold the other until the dead have returned.'

Hel bends close so that her face is centimetres from mine. A spider crawls out from her empty eye socket, then scuttles across her cheek and disappears into her jaw. She lifts the charm from my neck and whispers, 'Payment.'

I bite my lip and resist the urge to grab it back. I need it. It helps me find the ancient force inside me. But if I give it willingly, perhaps she will look kindly on me.

'And Stig?' I ask hopefully.

Hel spins around, her feathered cloak a tornado of destruction, and I glimpse the terrible power inside her: the power to strip flesh from bone and turn the living to dust.

She strides into the darkness. 'Return the dead and kill the *draugr*. A single, clean blow.'

Our Family Tree Is Twisted

I wake inside the chamber of the tree, under a blanket of moss and leaves. A grey-chested raven pecks and pulls at my wrist, and I blink in wonder as a root unwinds from my arm and slides across the ground, back into the hole behind me. The bird releases my other arm and flaps away with a caw. I sit up and groan. Everything hurts: my arms, my legs, my head.

Images flutter up from the back of my mind. A tattered cloak, an axe dripping with blood, a hollow eye socket . . . memories of a dream I can't stitch together.

Something jumps in my pocket and I feel a jolt of energy. The cord – I'm meant to use it to return Mormor and the rest of the dead. And then I have to . . . I rub my temples and try to remember. The axe . . . If I stop the creature, then maybe . . .

Stig.

My breath catches just to think his name. Hel said she hasn't called him to her yet. If I return the dead and kill the *draugr*, perhaps she will let him live. I push myself to my feet and step outside. As long as there is a shred of hope, I have to try.

The blizzard has stopped and snow sparkles in the sunshine. I wince against the glare, then hold my arm before me and search in every direction. I used to love the way snow makes everything new, but now the sweep of white seems sinister, as if deliberately hiding what went before.

My teeth won't stop chattering. I need to get indoors, and quickly. The cabin looks small and lonely on the other side of the garden; covered in snow, the plants on the roof take on strange shapes like weird topiary animals. I trudge towards it, straining for the slightest sound. I tell myself the creature won't come back, not when the sun is shining. It only appeared before when the light was low: twilight, fog, a blizzard. But that doesn't stop my body from tensing with dread.

As I walk, I scan the ground for Stig. I desperately want to see his face, but I couldn't bear it if . . . I push the thought of Yrsa and Olav away and force myself to move faster.

The cabin door is open. I pause, my heart pounding. Maybe Stig managed to crawl back. He might be inside, waiting for me.

I hurry up the path, then stop.

The door is wedged open with snow. Stig must have left it unlatched when he chased after me. The crust of ice is untouched: no footprints, no blood.

The axe is propped against the porch, where Stig left it. I grab it and march up the steps. Inside, the room is cold and grey. I kick out the worst of the snow, then close and bolt the door. Everything is just as before: the kitchen chair lying on the floor, the journals scattered on the rug. My gaze falls on Gandalf's empty bed and something inside me breaks.

He was so brave, he gave his life to save me. I wish he was here so I could hold him; so I could tell him he's a good boy. I wish he was here to lick my face.

The axe drops from my hand and my body heaves with sobs. All of me is shaking. I can't . . . can't stop. I wipe away my tears and tell myself to breathe. I *have* to survive to free Mormor and save Stig. I need to think straight. I need to get warm.

I wrap a blanket around myself, then kneel before the stove. My fingers fumble and I drop the matches. At last the spark takes. I glance at the window, dreading the sound of a howl but there's only the cry of the wind, whistling around the cabin like it's trying to get in.

It will be twilight soon. I need to be ready.

My gaze rests on the axe. There was a symbol, something I'm meant to do. I take a journal from the floor. There are lots of runes inside, but the words next to them mean nothing to me. I throw the book aside and pick up another. Why didn't I learn Norwegian? Mormor wanted to teach me, so why didn't I let her? Why didn't I ask more questions? I should have *made* Mum tell me the truth. I hurl the book and it slams into the wall.

I pace the cabin, chewing my thumbnail. What was it Stig said? Something about how Hel makes you see the good and bad in yourself . . . A memory pools at the back of my head. The things I don't want to feel; the person I don't want to be. I've been so full of self-pity, obsessed with hating the way I look – I pushed Stig away.

I didn't want to look into Hel's empty eye socket because I didn't want to see my own darkness reflected there. Mormor said a life can't be made up of summers, yet I only came to the island when it was permanently light – never when it was dark. I didn't want my happiness overshadowed by Mum and Mormor arguing. That's why I didn't force them to tell me the truth; that's why I didn't learn Norwegian. I didn't *want* to know what they were arguing about; I was happier pretending everything was OK.

My head feels clearer than it has in a long time. I may not be able to read Norwegian, but I *can* read clothing. My ancestors can speak to me through material. The doll is splayed out on the rug. I drop to my knees and snatch it up. Nothing. And then I remember. There was some fabric with the journals. I didn't look before because I was so focused on the books.

I grab the axe, then go to Mormor's room and lift

the lid of the chest. Inside is a roll of yellow-tinged material. I open it onto the bed, not caring about the smell. On the left is an embroidered trunk with dozens of branches. Under each one is a name and a date. Near the bottom is stitched 'Frida' – Mormor's name – and beneath it, nothing. I touch the space where Mum's name should be and my chest tightens. Because of her, our family tree is twisted. My fate distorted.

I look up and shiver. Shadows are swirling in the corners of the room. There's a dark mass behind the wardrobe, expanding and deflating, growing ever bigger. It reaches out to me, and I scramble to the middle of the bed.

Buzzing fills the air and I tell myself not to be afraid. *They didn't hurt you before . . .*

Unseen icy fingers close around mine. I watch helplessly as my hand is guided across the embroidery. It stops on the name Karina and the thought of her tugs at my mind, as if she's stitched a part of herself into the material. I reach for where my necklace should be and feel a pang of regret, but the thread pulls harder, demanding my focus.

A figure steps out from the shadows. She scowls a moment, then smiles. My shoulders drop with relief. I grin at her, then touch the next name – Gerd – and a tiny old lady with long flowing hair appears. I touch more names: Trine and Solveig and Astrid and Britt. My fingers trace the thread like a blind person reading Braille; each stitch tells a story at once familiar and strange.

More and more women appear, until I am surrounded. I look from face to face and my heart overflows with gratitude. They came back for me!

Karina points to the bed. There's a square of fabric next to the axe. It must have fallen out when I opened the roll of material. I turn it over to see a vertical line crossed by a diagonal one. The same symbol Hel showed me.

'Karina, what does it mean? What am I meant to do?' She replies in Norwegian.

I leap from the bed. 'But I don't understand!'

She tugs the fabric between my fingers and somehow I know that she has stitched it for me, for this moment. Taking a deep breath, I place my palm over the rune.

Karina intones a deep sound – 'Nau-dizzz' – that I've heard reverberate in my head before. The other women join her in a circle and the word becomes a chant, swirling around me as they raise their voices in a vortex of energy. I find I'm singing with them. My feet root themselves to the floor as courage rushes up through me, straightening my spine and expanding in my chest. I feel the strength of twenty women.

Suddenly I know what to do.

On Mormor's bedside table is an embroidery and a small pair of scissors. I take them and scratch the rune into the blade of the axe. Remembering what Hel showed me, I grit my teeth and pull the sharp edge across my palm. I wince in pain, then squeeze my hand and watch as blood drips onto the markings, making them glow white.

I look to Karina, hoping I have done enough, but her image is fading. The women's features have gone, just like they did after they created the bubble to save me from the *draugr*. Karina shakes her head, and I know that she cannot stay. I look around the circle and watch my ancestors disappear one by one, like light bulbs going out.

A Single, Clean Blow

I bandage my hand, then put on my gloves and pull the door shut. The sky is streaked purple and red, as if someone took a knife and slashed it open, the ghostly moon too afraid to show its face. Behind me, the cabin blazes with light. It spills out through the windows and onto the snow. A beacon.

Gripping the axe, I jump down the steps. The gnarled arms of the tree dip and wave as if beckoning me, and I hurry towards it. I have to return the dead before the *draugr* comes. If it kills me, there will be no one to save Mormor.

Two ravens circle high above, their bodies buffeted by the icy wind, and I am glad to see them. I pause at the edge of the garden, feeling exposed. If the creature appears now . . . A harsh caw sounds in warning and I glance in every direction, but there's nothing. I keep walking, the crunch of my boots horribly loud.

A howl comes from the forest.

My head spins as I stare about me. I turned on every light in the cabin to attract the *draugr*; if I go back it will find me . . . and the tree is too far.

The shed!

I turn and race towards it, then hurry inside. There are no windows and I have to strain to make out shapes in the gloom. My hand shakes as I pull the rusty bolt across.

Another howl, closer this time.

I want to hide in a corner, but I don't move. I need to know where it is. Shuffling sounds. A low, breathy snort.

It must be right outside.

My chest flushes with heat. I hold the axe before me, my hands sweating in my gloves.

The door rattles and I cry out, but it's just the wind.

Holding my breath, I peer through a crack in the wood. The yellow light from the cabin illuminates every weed stalk near the house, but there's no sign of the creature. I move my body to the left and angle my head to look to the other side.

A shape moves past, temporarily blocking the light.

I gasp and pull back, convinced it's seen me. When I look again, the creature is lumbering up the porch steps.

I slide open the bolt, ready.

It paces the porch, then looks in through the windows.

Bang. Bang. Bang.

It pounds its fist along the outside of the cabin. My fingers tighten around the axe, hatred burning inside me. A grunt, and then it kicks open the door and disappears inside.

Now. I have to go *now*.

I run to the tree, not daring to look back. My lungs burn as I gasp at the icy air. When I get near, the cord jumps in my pocket. I reach inside and stare in disbelief at the translucent, pulsating thing in my hands. It leaps to the ground, then lengthens to ten times its size and slithers towards the tree. I lurch forward and snatch it with both hands. The other end disappears into the hollow of the trunk, jolting my arms.

A thousand voices cry out. Shadowy faces rush past me at impossible speed. I bend my legs and brace my arms. The apparitions spin around the cord, then disappear into the tree with a whoosh and a crack. I shut my eyes and turn my head. Grit my teeth and hold on. Twice the cord twists in my hands and I nearly drop it. My arms shake. Still the dead come.

The whirlwind slows – ghostly faces continue to rush by but there are fewer now. There's no way to tell if Mormor is among them; I just have to hope.

I drop my shoulders and sigh. It's worked, the dead are returning.

My relief doesn't last long.

A figure stands on the other side of the tree. The

draugr. Its head jerks in my direction. With no ghostly army to hold it back it comes straight for me, its gait clumsy and lurching.

The cord tugs in my hands. The dead are still flowing into the underworld. If I let go now, they may never get back. I have to hold on.

The creature is close. Just twenty paces away.

I glance at the axe in the snow. With one hand holding the cord, I bend down and grab it. More ghostly faces rush past. I need both hands to fight, but I can't drop the cord. Not yet. I have to give the dead a chance to return.

And then I see her.

'Mormor!'

She stands halfway between me and the *draugr*, somehow managing to resist the pull of the cord. My heart wells with love. I gaze at her shimmering apparition and this time I know she can see me too. Her eyes gleam, as if she's illuminated from within.

I step towards her, wanting to say so much but unable to get the words out. All I manage is a half-sobbed, 'I love you, Mormor.'

She smiles and gives me the tender look I'm so familiar with – the one that tells me not to upset myself. I don't have to explain because she already knows.

'Yes, child. I'm here. I love you too, more than you can imagine.'

She moves towards me, her smile radiating kindness. I long to touch her, but I'm afraid to drop the axe or the cord. She's so close. I reach out my hand . . .

The *draugr* howls.

Mormor turns her back to me and squares up to the creature.

'Mormor, no! Please, you have to go back to the underworld!'

She glances over her shoulder. 'I will never leave you, child.'

'For me, Mormor. *Please*. I can't hold the cord much longer!'

The caw of a raven sounds from above.

'I have Odin's ravens with me. I'm not alone. You can leave me. You *must!*'

Mormor steps towards the *draugr*. The creature tilts its head back and a strange bark issues from its mouth. It's laughing.

I call to Mormor, 'Go to the underworld and we can be together one day!' My voice breaks with emotion. 'Please, Mormor. Or I'll never see you again.'

Mormor stands firm. If she isn't going to move, I'll have to make her.

I throw the rope towards her. It latches onto her wrist then snakes around her middle, grasping her in its coil. I mouth, *I'm sorry*, and then she's gone, pulled with the cord into the tree. My chest aches with longing as I stare after her.

Seeing her, even for a brief moment, gives me courage. I grip the axe as the *draugr* circles around me. It paces slowly to the right, its yellow eyes never leaving my face. Then grunts and snorts, coming closer and backing away. Testing me. Playing with me.

It rushes to the left, and I spin around and lift the axe . . . but it's too fast. Its body slams into me and knocks me to the ground. Pain rips through my right shoulder. I cry out and gasp for breath.

The axe!

I lurch for it, but the *draugr* steps on the handle, pushing it into the snow. Desperate, I search the ground for a fallen branch, anything.

One of the ravens flies close to my head and caws, 'Naudiz!'

I reach for my *valknut* charm and panic when I realise it's not there.

'Naudiz!' I yell the word, but nothing happens.

A clawed hand grabs my wrist and a harsh, guttural sound rasps from the creature's mouth. I don't understand the words it spits at me, but I can feel the hatred behind them. The *draugr* twists my arm and pain shoots through my shoulder, causing lights to flash before my eyes. I cry out in agony and drop to my knees.

Weak and hopeless, I hang my head and whisper, 'I'm sorry, Stig. I tried.'

A raucous caw makes me lift my gaze. A raven dives from the sky. His eyes are pure rage: burning black dots ringed by fire. Mighty wings beat the air as he claws the creature's head. The *draugr* drops my wrist to bat at the bird. It attacks again, diving and pecking at the creature's hands, its face, its eyes.

I push myself up and another raven lands heavily on my shoulder. 'Naudiz!' it calls. The bird explodes into the sky, then wheels through the air and joins the attack.

I have to try again. Remembering how it felt when my ancestors chanted, I take a deep breath and feel my feet become rooted to the earth. My legs tremble as I reach into the deepest part of me, willing the energy to surge up my spine and into my chest. When I can't hold it any longer, I open my mouth.

'Nau-dizzz!'

The deep sound resonates through my body and shakes the branches of the tree. I sound the word again. This time even louder. The third time I vibrate the rune's name, a mass of silver threads appears in the air. I stare at the *draugr* and focus my energy on it. The threads attach themselves to one another to form a net. I will them forward and they wrap around the creature, encasing its upper body.

The *draugr* howls. It staggers but stays upright, its arms bound to its sides. I take the axe from the snow. Ignoring the pain in my shoulder, I prepare to strike.

A single, clean blow.

I look down and notice a black shape struggling in the net. The *draugr's* fingers are clasped around the raven's neck – it must have grabbed the bird before the threads closed around it. The other raven desperately pecks at the silver cage, trying to release it.

If I kill the *draugr* now, one of the birds may die.

I lower the axe, then carefully use the blade to slice open the threads. They ping back as if made of metal, and the raven bursts out. I start to say the rune again, but the *draugr* rips the net wide and smacks me across the face. I stumble back, tasting blood.

Fear rises to my chest but I push it back down. It's no good running. I need to fight it – but I need an advantage, some way to outsmart it.

The ravens fly into the branches of the tree, which gives me an idea. I chase after the birds, the *draugr* close behind. As I get near, I see the tree is covered with dozens of ravens, sitting on its branches like dark assassins.

I point towards the creature and scream, 'Kill it!'

Raucous caws fill the air as they explode upward and then dive, black wings shattering the sky. I look back and the *draugr*'s head, arms and legs are covered in the birds. It throws them off and staggers forward, but more come down. Razor-sharp beaks stab at its eyes. Claws rip chunks of its skin and hair. The attack is frenzied and relentless.

Bending almost double, I clamber inside the hollow trunk of the tree. The ground is covered with dead leaves and it smells of dank wood and rot. I blink against the gloom and try not to think about the hole to the underworld.

There isn't enough room to swing an axe, but if the *draugr* follows me inside, maybe I can hide by the other exit of the chamber and kill it as it emerges.

I go to the far opening, opposite to where I entered, and bury the axe under a pile of leaves in case the *draugr* tries to take it. If it thinks I'm unarmed, I'll have the advantage of surprise. I hurry back to the middle of the space and wait. My heart beats like a wild thing. I turn and stare to my left, presuming the creature will follow the way I came, then check to the right just in case. The only sound is my breathing and the caw of the birds.

A voice calls in the distance. I'm sure I heard my name. I listen but there's nothing. Maybe it was just the wind.

'Martha!'

This time there's no mistake. Mum!

I rush to the opening of the tree but I can't see her. Maybe she's gone to the forest, or back to the cabin? I want to call out, but what if she comes and the creature is waiting? I couldn't bear it if –

Something grabs my hair and forces me down. My face scrapes the ground as I'm dragged backwards. The *draugr* grunts and snorts behind me. I struggle onto my back. The creature's nose is missing, so that there's just a hole. A large scrap of skin hangs from its face, its head mostly just skull. The ravens have pecked its shoulders clean to the bone.

I kick as hard as I can. Managing to get free, I hurry to the right side of the chamber. I search the leaves but I can't find the axe! My fingers dig into the leaves and earth. Shaking with panic, I run to the other exit, then come back. At last I find it.

Too late. The *draugr* is before me, just outside the tree. It must have gone out the other way and around the outside. It reaches in to grab me, when something slams into its head and it stumbles sideways. Mum stands behind the creature, holding a branch.

'Mum!'

She sees me and nods, then readies herself to strike again. Her pale face is set with grim determination. I can't believe she's here – and fighting! I grab the axe and scramble out from the tree. Once outside, I hurl the weapon on top of a massive gnarled root, then clamber after it. Bracing my legs, I raise the axe with both hands.

Mum stumbles, the *draugr* almost on her. She screams in fright and I point to the other entrance. A flash of understanding crosses her face, and she runs around the side of the trunk, the creature close behind. I steady my feet and balance my weight. Tensing my arms, I take a deep breath. My timing has to be perfect, I have to get it right.

Mum emerges from the tree beneath me and staggers away from the opening, then collapses with a sob.

The bone of an arm appears, followed by a head.

Summoning my strength, I lift the axe and swing.

NO MORE SECRETS

I stumble down from the tree, and Mum is there with her arms outstretched. She holds me close. 'Thank God you're OK.' I close my eyes and my body trembles with relief. The fibres of her duffel coat speak of fear, but also of determination and great love. She collapses in my arms and I haul her back to her feet.

The sky is dark now, with only the moon to see by. We steady each other, and she points and says, 'What the hell *was* that thing?' I glance at the grotesque severed head and bury my face in her shoulder. The creature's body lies half inside the hollow of the tree. Dozens of ravens caw and flap over it, sharp beaks feasting on the last scraps of sinew and skin.

'It killed Yrsa and Olav!'

Mum pulls away from me. 'What?'

'We found them dead in the snow.'

'Who is we?'

'Stig. He should be here, but I don't even know if he's alive.'

Fear crowds my mind as I remember Hel's words. She didn't promise to let Stig live. But I returned the dead and killed the *draugr*, so maybe . . . Staggering into the dark, I take a few paces one way and then another. 'Stig!' I run wildly, ignoring Mum's pleas to come back.

The ravens flap and caw above me, and then land to my right. I run to them and see a mound in the snow. Please. Please, let him be OK.

Stig's face is blue. His cheek feels like ice, yet the only wound I can see is a faint pink scar on his neck. 'Stig! Wake up!' I call his name over and over, but he doesn't open his eyes.

A hand touches my shoulder. I look up and see Mum. She takes off a glove and holds a finger to his throat. 'There's a pulse. Quick.'

We reach under his armpits and haul him up. Somehow we manage to drag him between us. He murmurs something and my heart soars. 'It's OK, Stig,' I whisper. 'We've got you. Everything's going to be OK, I promise.'

Mum glances at me over his head, as if she's not so sure.

In the cabin, we lay him on the sofa.

'Blankets, quickly!'

I rush to Mormor's room and drag the cover from the bed, then go to the spare room and take another. Returning to the lounge, I throw them on the sofa and help Mum remove Stig's coat and boots.

She tucks the blankets around him, then notices my worried face. 'He needs to warm up. Give it a few minutes.' She shakes her head and sighs. 'That thing outside – I've seen it in visions, but I never believed –'

'Visions?'

'Hallucinations . . . I used to paint the images to get them out of my head.'

Mum touches Stig's forehead. She rubs his arm and I do the same.

'Once I started the medication, I hoped the visions would stop, but they didn't. And then you had the accident. If only I had –' She takes a deep breath. 'The doctors say I didn't foresee what happened, they say it was a false memory that I created after the event, but the images kept coming. In every one was the tree. I knew I had to keep you away from it.'

She rubs her temples and glances at Stig. His skin is more white than blue now, and his breathing is shallow but regular. If only he would open his eyes.

'Just before you went, I started to get a new vision. I kept painting that . . . that *thing* outside.'

Mormor said there have been many seers in the family. Maybe Mum painted the *draugr* for the same reason my ancestors did those charcoal drawings: to warn of what was to come.

'Is that why you told me to leave the cabin?'

221

She nods and a lump comes to my throat. 'We tried, Mum! We were going to Olav and Yrsa's, but we found them dead in the snow. They'd been clawed to death.'

Mum's face is ashen. She looks at me, unsure, then swallows hard. 'I'll drive to the police station later. First I need to know what's been happening. And I mean *everything*.'

Stig's eyes flutter open. I wrap my arms around his neck. 'You're OK!' I pull away and look at him, but there's something wrong. His eyes are dark and vacant, like he's not really inside.

'Mum?'

'Give it a few minutes, Martha.' Mum tries to sound reassuring, but I can tell she's worried too.

Stig turns his head to one side and groans. Maybe Hel let him live but he's just a shell – or worse, a creature like the *draugr*. His mouth parts and he licks his lips. He opens his eyes and briefly looks at me, then stares over my shoulder as if he's seen someone he recognises. 'Nina?' he croaks. My heart twists. Mum gives me a quizzical look and I shake my head. Why would he say *her* name?

He mutters something in Norwegian and I turn to Mum, wanting her to translate. She touches my arm and shakes her head. 'He's confused.'

Maybe Mum is right, he doesn't know what he's saying. A long minute passes, and then Stig blinks at me and smiles. There is so much warmth in his gaze that my doubt and fear melt away. 'You're OK?'

He gives the smallest nod and I hug him, my heart

expanding in my chest until there's no room for anything but love. He still feels so cold though. I hold him tightly, trying to share my warmth with him.

Mum stands and looks at Stig, then back to me. 'Aren't you going to introduce us?'

I touch his shoulder, 'Mum, this is Stig.'

Mum takes off her coat. 'Yes, I've gathered this is Stig. I'll make us all a hot drink, and then you can tell me *who* Stig is and what's been happening here, OK?' Mum shakes her head and mutters, 'Even poor Gandalf looks worn out.'

'Gandalf!'

He's curled up in his bed with his head on his paws. I rush to him and kneel by his side. 'But I thought . . . !' He licks my face and my heart fills with gratitude. I give him the biggest hug, and then pat his head and whisper, 'Good boy. Thank you, thank you, thank you.'

Mum busies herself in the kitchen. She turns on the tap and fills the kettle, then opens a cupboard and sighs. 'Where's the coffee gone?'

Stig whispers hoarsely, 'Top shelf, red tin,' and I grin at him, wanting to absorb every detail of his face. The way his dimples appear slowly and then all at once when he smiles. The deep crease in his bottom lip that's so kissable. I touch his feet through the pile of blankets and find a toe to hold. He grins and I smile back so hard my cheeks ache. I can't wait for us to be alone together. There's so much I want to say.

Mum grabs my arm and steers me into the kitchen.

I brace myself for the talk – the one where she tells me off for running away and freaks out about the goth on the sofa. Instead she takes a shaky breath and murmurs, 'I should have told you about Mormor.'

I stare at her in surprise, a familiar tightness in my chest. I'm angry that she lied, but she was so brave, charging in and bashing the creature with that branch. I know she would do anything for me. She didn't tell me about Mormor's funeral because she knew I would insist on coming here, and she wanted to keep me away from the tree. She was trying to protect me.

Mum pours boiling water into the coffee pot. 'No more secrets, I promise. But I need to know what's been going on.' She stirs the coffee and then pours three cups and hands me one. I follow her into the living room to find Stig snoring softly. She places a drink on the floor next to him and shoos me back to the kitchen, as if she knows I could happily stand and watch him sleep.

I sit at the table and wrap my hands around my cup. The coffee is hot and delicious, even better than how Mormor used to make it. Maybe staring death in the face does that to you – makes everything taste better and feel more alive.

Mum raises her eyebrows. 'Well?'

I take a deep breath. 'You know how Mormor wanted you to water the tree? Well, no one did and it started to rot.'

Mum looks at me blankly. 'And?'

'Beneath its roots is the underworld. A hole formed and the dead escaped.'

Mum's eyes widen.

'That thing I killed was a *draugr*.'

She stares into her cup. 'Your grandmother showed me a chest of journals once. She said there are mystical beings who live in the tree. She took me out there and told me to listen, but it was all nonsense.'

'Mormor was telling the truth, Mum – about everything.'

She buries her face in her hands. 'Oh my God, I didn't believe her. I thought it was some weird obsession, or maybe she'd been hallucinating and it must run in the family.'

My jaw tenses with resentment. If Mum had done her duty and watered the tree, none of this would have happened. Why couldn't she just have believed Mormor?

I go to the window and a thought drops into my mind like the last piece of a jigsaw. 'You read the letters Mormor sent to me before you burned them, didn't you?' Mum hangs her head and I continue, 'You knew I could read clothing. You could have told me it had happened to you too, but you didn't.'

Mum gives me a pained look. 'I heard a voice at the tree once, or thought I did. Your dad and I were having problems and I was under a lot of strain. Afterwards, I could sense things when I touched people's clothes, but the way the doctor explained it, it all made sense. I'd latched onto the idea of being able to read clothing because your grandmother had told me about it so many times.'

She takes a shaky breath. 'If I had known you would come out here by yourself, I would have told you everything, believe me.' Mum wipes her eyes, then stands and walks over to me. She speaks slowly, as if it's hard for her to get the words out. 'I'm sorry I burned the letters. I'm sorry I kept everything from you.'

I don't say anything and she sighs. 'I didn't want Mormor to fill your head with the same nonsense. I didn't want you to become like me!'

I glance at the window, where our reflections stare back at us from the glass. We look so similar. I wonder why I've never noticed before. I don't know whether to be angry or feel sorry for her.

I touch her arm and her woolly jumper is heavy with fear and confusion. She found it easier to believe that she'd been hallucinating than admit that there's magic in the world. She's been trapped for so long, afraid to admit the truth. I am disappointed in her, but then I know how easy it is to delude yourself. I was so absorbed by self-pity that I convinced myself Stig couldn't be interested in me. I shudder, remembering the nightmare I had, where my eyes and mouth were stitched up. If I hadn't seen how I was, that would have been my fate – cut off from the world; sewn shut.

'I will tell you everything, but first you have to read the journals. OK?'

Mum takes a moment. 'OK.'

A weight I didn't know I had been carrying lifts from my shoulders. I feel so tired. My head spins and I grip the counter to stop myself falling.

'Are you all right, Martha? Maybe you should lie down.'

She leads me into the lounge. 'I'll go to the police in the morning. You can tell me where Yrsa and Olav are, and I'll say I found them while I was walking the dog. That way you won't have to lie when you give a statement.'

'Thanks, Mum.'

There is so much I have to say, but I'm so tired. Tired of feeling angry and disappointed. With everything that's happened, it doesn't seem important. She loves me and she's here for me now, and that's what matters.

I stop at the sofa and take a long, blissful look at Stig. I wish I could stay by his side all night. 'Mum, will you watch him for me, make sure he's OK?'

'Of course. Now into bed.'

A Tiny Knock at the Door

I wake to the sound of a happy house: people talking and laughing. For a moment I don't dare open my eyes. Stig is alive. Mum is here and she knows the truth. Gandalf is fine. It's like when I used to wake on Christmas morning and was afraid to explore the house.

In the kitchen, Stig has his back to me, eating breakfast, and Mum is at the sink. The two of them are chatting happily in Norwegian. I go to Stig and hug him around the neck, cautious of his wound even though it seems healed. He smiles at me and I grin back.

Feeling uncomfortable with Mum in the room, I look at the pile of journals on the table. Her reading glasses sit on top of them and I wonder how many she's read and how much she knows.

Mum sees me and smiles. 'Breakfast?'

'Great. I'm starving.'

I sit opposite Stig and she sets a plate of pancakes and a cup of coffee before me.

'Good?' asks Stig.

I swallow. 'Very. But not as good as yours.'

'I heard that, young lady.' Mum sits next to me. 'When you've finished, I thought we might take a walk out to the tree and water it together. And then you can tell me where . . .'

I nod, not wanting to think about Yrsa and Olav. I point at the journals. 'So you read them?'

'Yes, and Stig told me some of what's been happening. It's a lot to take in.'

Stig smiles shyly. 'It was for me too. I didn't believe Martha at first; it seemed so crazy. I found it hard to trust, but she has a way of being persuasive.'

I smile at Stig and feel so many things. Happy and excited that I met him and he's OK, but sad about Yrsa and Olav.

After we clear the breakfast things, we put on our coats and head out. I trudge through the snow with Stig and Gandalf, while Mum strides out, carrying the pail. She slows as we reach the tree and I gaze at its mighty branches and imagine Odin hanging above me, finding the runes in the well. My breath catches, remembering what Stig said. If the journals are right, the tree stands at the centre of the cosmos, connecting different worlds. Who knows where its branches and roots might lead?

Mum's face is pale. I leave Stig and take her arm. 'I

used to be afraid of it too.' I realise that it no longer scares me. The dead are back where they belong and there's nothing that remains of the *draugr* – not even bones. The ravens must have carried them away. As long as we tend to the tree, it should never happen again.

Mum watches as I take the pail from her, dip it in the well, then throw the water over the hole inside the tree. A raven caws overhead and she glances nervously at the sky.

'It's fine, Mum, I promise. Nothing bad is going to happen.'

'OK. I might leave you two alone. I've got some more reading to do.'

She spots the axe in the snow and picks it up. I give her a hug and watch as she trudges back to the cabin with it. Stig stares at the tree, seemingly lost in thought.

'Penny for them.'

'What?'

'For your thoughts. It means, what are you thinking?'

'Oh.' Stig puts an arm around me and pulls me close. I fall into him, enjoying his warmth.

'Sprinkler systems,' he says.

'What?'

'I know you need to water the roots every day, but there's no reason why you need to use the pail, is there?'

Gandalf comes over and wags his tail as if he thinks it's a good idea.

I laugh and Stig looks at me in surprise. 'What's funny? I think it could work!'

I wrap my arm around his waist. 'No, you're right.'

He turns and leans close, and I hold my breath as his lips meet mine. He kisses me again and again, each one a tiny knock at the door of my heart. The softness of him melts every part of me. I feel like a thread unravelling, coming undone. Being with him, kissing him here under the tree, feels so right.

Stig pulls away and stares at something behind me.

I follow his gaze. 'Something wrong?'

'I thought I saw . . .' He takes my hand and squeezes it tight. 'When you see the dead, how do they appear?'

I glance at him, surprised. 'Can we talk about it another time?'

'Sure, sure.' A look I know so well passes across his face – a dark cloud then sunshine. A flicker of emotion, followed by its opposite.

He yanks my arm. 'Come on, before my nose freezes off!'

We walk back to the cabin hand in hand. There are so many things we don't know about each other that our conversation jumps all over the place. I want to ask him about all his likes and dislikes, the places he's been and the things he's seen. I have a million questions.

As we climb the porch steps I stop and kiss him again. I don't know which I want to do more, talk or kiss. The thought makes me laugh.

He pinches me lightly on the nose. 'What's funny?'

'I was just thinking of all the kissing and talking I want to do. I don't know how I'm going to fit it all in. Even ten lifetimes wouldn't be enough.'

Stig flashes me his dimples. '*Du er deilig*. And we have plenty of time, don't worry.'

I try to smile, but I can't help worrying. What if Mum insists that we go home right away – what will happen to Stig? How will I get to see him?

Inside, Mum is drying up at the sink. The cabin feels so different – the emptiness and the shadows have gone. It looks how I remember: a place where I was happy.

She turns and gives me a knowing smile, then narrows her eyes. I know I'm going to have to answer a lot of questions about Stig, as well as everything else. Things might be tough for a while – I'm going to have to help Mum get her head around things. It should have been her supporting me, but that's just how it is. We have to work together now.

I shrug out of my coat and hang it over a chair, but I misjudge the distance and it drops to the floor. Stig grabs it for me and I smile a thank-you, glad of his help.

Mum coughs. 'I've been thinking – I could sell the house in London and move here.'

Stig looks at Mum expectantly, then takes himself off to sit by the stove. I haven't thought about the future properly. Maybe I've been purposefully avoiding it – not wanting to think about how Stig and I will be together exactly, just hoping that we would.

'We can both live here together,' I say.

Mum frowns. 'You don't have to stay out here with me. Watering the tree is my responsibility.'

'But I want to be here with you and Stig!'

'You're seventeen, Martha. You have your education to think about. I'm sure you can stay with Dad. If you don't want to go to school, we can arrange some kind of home tutor.'

'But, Mum, I can get the ferry to a college on the mainland. Some of them must offer classes in English – and anyway, I want to learn Norwegian.'

Mum raises an eyebrow.

It's only been a few days since I left home, but so much has changed. Whatever happens with Stig and me, I don't want to hide away any more. And I need to learn Norwegian so I can read the journals for myself.

'If you're sure.' Mum smiles and I wrap my arms around her. Her yellow chiffon scarf crackles with energy. Chiffon holds a person's daydreams, and an image comes to me now: she's standing in a large sunlit room, teaching students to paint.

Mum used to sell her paintings at a major art gallery in London, but she stopped around the time Dad left. I used to love going to her openings; I was so proud of how talented she is. She's never mentioned wanting to teach, but I think she'd be brilliant at it. A shiver of excitement runs through me. Dad signed over the house to her after the divorce. It must be worth a lot – easily enough to get something out here.

'Mum, there's an old guest house for sale by the harbour. What about doing it up and running an artists' retreat? The light there is amazing and so are the views.'

'I don't know. It would be a lot of work.'

I point at Stig, who is throwing a log on the fire, but she only frowns in reply. Stig could help do the place up; I know he could. It would be fun to meet new people. Maybe I could take their coats at the door and then use my gift to help them make the right decisions in life, so they don't die with regrets. The idea of using my gift to help people feels right somehow.

Mum lowers her voice. 'It's too soon, Martha. Besides, you barely know him.' She sees my face and her voice softens. 'Look, we'll talk about it later. We don't have to decide anything right now.'

I nod, but I'm already thinking about packing up my things in London. Though I'll miss Stig, I can't wait to see Kelly. I won't mention the walking corpse I beheaded, but I know she'll want to hear all about my boyfriend.

Stig is tending the fire, his back to me. He must be able to hear our conversation, so why isn't he saying anything? Mum pipes up before I can stop her. 'So what are your plans, Stig?' I glare at her, my heart in my mouth.

He turns around and smiles. 'I need to go to Oslo. Just for a few days. I need to talk to Mum, but then I'm coming back here to look for work.'

My heart falters. If he goes home, does that mean he will see his ex-girlfriend? What if he mentioned her name because he's still in love with her? The words slip out before I can stop myself. 'Will you see Nina?'

Stig glances anxiously at the window. When he speaks his voice sounds far away. 'Yes. I need to know if she woke up from the coma.'

Something drops inside me, like a pebble sinking into a well. 'But before, you said that she –'

He forces a smile. 'I'll be back soon. Don't worry.'

Stig walks over and lays a hand on my shoulder, and part of me wants to flinch from his touch. He smiles into my eyes and I feel the brush of his coat sleeve. Anger, hatred and jealousy burn into me, followed by love and kindness. The same emotions I felt before, in the woodshed. I thought it was his dad I was picking up, but what if . . .

'Martha?'

Stig looks at me expectantly. How can I doubt him, after all we've been through?

I grab the journals from the table, happy to find an excuse to leave the room. 'I'm going to put these back.'

Hugging the books to myself, I watch Stig wander over to the fire. He sits on the floor, then takes out his phone and grins, and I wonder who has messaged him. Or maybe he's looking at photos. When I turn back, Mum gives me a suspicious look. Ignoring her raised eyebrows, I head to Mormor's room and shut the door.

A PRETTY GIRL SMILES BACK

I drop the journals on the bed, then stand at the window. Snowflakes swirl together and flutter to the ground. At first just a few, and then the world is disguised by a veil of white. The snow settles quickly, hiding the past with a fresh layer of white.

Before, Stig said Nina had woken up from the coma and is fine. Why tell me that if she hadn't? What else is he lying about? As much as I hate to admit it, Mum is right. I don't really know him.

A tap at the door makes me jump. What if it's Stig? I lick my lips, my mouth suddenly dry. Maybe I shouldn't say anything; I don't want him to think I don't trust him.

My voice sounds unsure. 'Come in.'

It's Mum. She closes the door behind her. 'You OK?'

I nod, and she sits on the bed and gestures to the pile of journals and material. 'I take it this lot was in the chest?'

'Uh-huh.'

She points to the roll of material. 'What's that?'

I open it out. 'Our family tree.'

Her eyes widen as she studies it. 'The numbers though, they can't be birthdates. Mormor's birthday is in April.'

I glance at her face, wondering how much to tell her. 'I think it might be when our ancestors met the Norns; when they were first able to read clothing.'

Mum touches one of the embroidered names and snatches back her hand.

Excitement rises inside me. 'Did you feel something?'

'I . . . I don't know. It was like someone calling to me through the thread.'

She seems scared, and I wish she wasn't. I'd love to be able to share the experience with someone, with her. 'It's weird at first, but you get used to it, honestly. Try touching it again. See what else you feel.'

'No.' She rubs her head, then adds, 'I thought it was just clothes, not fabric.'

'It is only clothes. It doesn't happen with ordinary material, but I think . . .' I chew my thumbnail. She probably doesn't want to hear about ghosts; that bit can wait for later. 'I think our ancestors can speak to us through their work. It's like they've stitched their intent into the fabric and we're following the thread back to them.'

Mum looks at me warily. I sit next to her and go to touch her arm, but she flinches. My hurt must be written across my face, because she instantly softens. 'I'm sorry. I don't know why I did that.'

Swallowing my disappointment, I look at the embroidered tree and wish things were easier between us. Mormor always seemed to understand. She knew without words, but then she could read my thoughts and emotions from my clothing. If I had known, I might have felt differently about wanting to hug her. I decide not to take Mum's reaction personally. 'Have you noticed there's a gap under Mormor's name?' I ask.

Mum stands and turns her back to me. I feel stupid suddenly. What was I thinking? That she would give me a sewing lesson and we'd happily stitch our names together, and then add a few flowers and a rainbow?

Mum heads to the door. 'Maybe later, OK?' She turns, as if something has just occurred to her. 'I know the date . . . when the Norns first appeared to me, I mean.' I look at her in surprise, thinking she wouldn't want to talk about it.

'It was four years ago, on the last day of August. I know because that's the day your dad phoned and said he wouldn't be there when we got home to England.'

Mum takes a deep breath. 'You know, the worst thing about the divorce is feeling that I've failed you.'

'Failed me?'

'I didn't want you to come from a broken home. I shouldn't have stuck by him after the first affair, but I thought he'd change after you were born.'

I never realised Mum felt that way, or that Dad had cheated on her before, though somehow it doesn't surprise me. I think back on all the birthdays and sports days he wasn't there for. Though I miss him sometimes, he spent so much time working away. He always had one foot in our life, the other out of it. 'You're not responsible for Dad. He's his own person. I think he's been seeing Chantelle a lot longer than he admits too.'

Mum smiles, a look of relief on her face.

I glance back at the embroidery. The stitching is so impressive. Each tiny knot and twig of the tree perfectly captured.

Mum sees me looking. 'I'll give our ancestors one thing: they were good with a needle and thread.'

I pick up the wonky heart-shaped cushion I made as a kid. 'Beats my efforts.'

Mum grabs the cushion and hits me with it. 'Who cares? You have other talents.'

'I'm handy with an axe, you mean?'

Mum laughs, and it reminds me of how she used to be. I'm glad to see her happy.

'So this Stig, you like him?'

I nod, unsure what to say. I do like him, *so* much. I want to tell her about the whole Nina thing, but I don't feel ready. Not when I don't know what to think myself.

'Well, any boy would be lucky to have you.'

She opens the door and gives me a big smile, the kind that says everything will be all right.

Once she's gone, I walk to the window. Maybe it's the hypnotic nature of the falling snow, but I find myself staring into space, thinking about everything that's happened.

A flash of movement catches my attention. I only caught a glimpse, but it looked like the ghost I saw in the cabin – the girl with short dark hair, wearing a shift dress. I press my palm to the cold glass. It can't be! And then I remember how I dropped the cord because I wanted to make sure Mormor went back to the underworld. What if I let go too soon?

I pick up a journal from the bed and flick through it, sure I've seen her face before. And then it comes to me. The photo on Stig's phone: the girl on the trapeze wire. Nina!

A chasm opens up within me and dark thoughts rush inside.

When I saw her before, I thought she was glaring accusingly at me, but what if she was looking at Stig? He said he'd been helping her train – maybe he was the one who didn't do up her harness properly. He was so jumpy when Yrsa knocked on the door; perhaps he *is* on the run.

I drop to the bed, my mind whirling. When I touched Stig's rag of regret, it tried to show me something about Nina, but I didn't want to see. As soon as Stig opened his eyes, he said her name. What if he saw her ghost; she might be haunting him because she wants revenge.

Stig's coat held such anger, but that was his dad,

not him. I'm sure Stig wouldn't hurt anyone. A familiar ache spreads in my chest. I wish Mormor were here. She would know what to do. I can almost hear her voice, urging me to trust my instincts and speak to him. My shoulders drop with relief; my decision is made. Before Stig leaves for Oslo, I will make him tell me the truth. Whatever it is, it's better to know.

Determined to put it out of my head, I open the door to Mormor's wardrobe and smile to see her bunad. It was always special to her. She wore it on her birthday and special occasions, and if I begged enough, she'd put it on just to make me grin.

I reach for the wooden hanger, careful to avoid touching the material, and lay it out on the bed. There's a white blouse, over which sits a blue bodice and a full skirt embroidered with colourful flowers. Seeing it fills me with sadness, but thinking about the times she wore it makes me happy too.

I touch the costume and see a girl with long blonde hair, no older than six, clapping her hands as her grandmother dances under the tree, twirling her long skirt. The girl is me! Joy fills my chest as I see myself through Mormor's eyes. The love she feels for me is so profound, so perfect.

I watch in wonder as Mormor puts her shawl around the girl's shoulders and takes her hands. 'What do you hear?' she asks. The girl closes her eyes. She doesn't see the raven that circles above, then lands on a branch to watch her. Nor does she see the three women that hold hands in a circle. But Mormor does.

She sees them like she always does, and it makes her smile.

The girl opens her eyes and Mormor tells her, 'The fates have a special purpose for you, my child. Keep listening and one day you shall hear them.'

I pull my hand away and open my eyes. Mormor said her bunad would be mine one day. Now seems like the right time. I change into the outfit and a feeling of comfort and warmth envelops me, as if Mormor is hugging me through the material. I plait my hair how Mormor used to wear hers, then put a dab of her perfume on my neck.

I stand and appraise myself in the mirror, turning this way and that, looking at my slim waist in the tight-fitting bodice and feeling the skirt swish around my legs. The only thing missing is my necklace. I feel sad for a moment, but then I realise that I don't need it; Odin's power is in my veins, not in a charm – and besides, I can always make another. I smile at myself and a pretty girl smiles back.

Peering into the chest, I see a single notebook. I pick it up and sit with it on my lap, thinking about all the women with the same gift as me who have written journals, telling their stories for the next generation of women to find.

Inside the book, the pages are blank. I reach for the pocket of my rucksack and take out a pen. Hel is right – it's time for me to write my own story.

THE END

Author's Note

Choosing names for my characters is one of my favourite jobs as an author. I love researching the meaning behind them and can't start writing until I find one that feels just right. In case you're wondering, here's why I chose the names I did.

Aslaug is a queen consort in Norse mythology. Derived from Old Norse (prefix *áss-*, meaning 'god', and suffix *-laug*, meaning 'betrothed woman'), the regal name seemed a fitting choice for the woman who started such a magical ancestral line.

Gandalf is a nod to Odin, via *The Lord of the Rings*. Gandalf the wizard was very much inspired by the Norse god of magic. In a letter dated 1946, Tolkien writes that he thought of Gandalf as an Odinic wanderer – a man who bore a spear or staff and wore a cloak and a wide-brimmed hat. Odin, of course, wore his hat with one side pulled low to disguise his missing eye.

There are lots more similarities – both figures are carried by a special horse, can understand the language of birds and beasts and are associated with ravens, eagles and wolves. As Martha named Mormor's dog, the suggestion is that she's always felt drawn to the fictional wizard/Odin.

As well as being grey (like Gandalf the Grey and Odin Grey Beard), my Gandalf is brave and loyal and willing to make the ultimate sacrifice for his friends. I've always had the feeling he knows a lot more than the average dog, so I wouldn't be surprised if he was quite magical too.

Martha is just a name I like; I didn't choose it consciously. It's always struck me as sounding fairly humble, and Martha's journey is about stepping into her power. Interestingly, the Marthas in *The Handmaid's Tale* are housemaids – women who wear dull colours and toil in the background. In the Bible, Martha was the sister of Lazarus and known for her obsession with housework. The name means 'lady' or 'mistress of the house'.

Mormor is Norwegian for grandmother. It translates as 'mother's mother'.

Olav is a fairly common name in Norway, and I wanted an 'everyman' feel for the character of Olav. Perhaps it's because of Olaf in Disney's *Frozen* (also set in

Norway), but the name makes me think of a friendly face – which is what Olav is for Martha.

Stig is a Scandinavian name that derives from the word *stiga*, meaning 'wanderer' – an ideal choice for a runaway. I also like the subtle nod to Odin, the ultimate wanderer, who journeys through the worlds carrying a traveller's staff.

Yrsa is said to derive from an ancient Norse word for 'she-bear'. Other sources suggest it comes from the Old Norse feminine name Ýrr, which is derived from the Old Norse *œrr*, meaning 'mad, furious, wild'. The character of Yrsa is formidable in every way, so this seemed a perfect choice for her.

Acknowledgements

First and foremost, a heartfelt thank you to my writing mentor, Lee Weatherly. A talented author, Lee is also one of the best in the business at assessing other writers' manuscripts. Luckily for me, she's also a wonderfully kind human being – the type to take in a puppy abandoned in a foreign country and a stray writer with the dream of one day being published. Without Lee's expert editorial eye, support and generosity, this book would not exist.

I must also thank my dear friend Maddy Elruna, a gifted shaman and tarot reader who introduced me to the Norse gods. Her belief, passion and dedication to Hel and the Norns inspired me to write this story and she has been a constant source of encouragement throughout my journey to publication.

Thank you to the team at Hot Key Books for making me feel so very welcome, and for the gentle and insightful guidance of my editor Felicity Johnston and the keen eye of copy editor Talya Baker. Thanks to Mathilde Skjerpen Fongen for her translation work in helping to ensure the narrative is authentic as possible, and to Rohan Eason for illustrating the front cover and Cherie Chapman for the book design.

I'm hugely grateful to my ever-patient agent, Amber Caraveo of Skylark Literary. Genuinely passionate about books, super-sharp and thorough to a fault, I could not ask for better.

I also owe a debt of gratitude to my very many beta readers (the Goodreads community is amazing!) for reading early versions of this book and my other writing projects. Also my SCBWI critique group and the Lewes Snowdrop Writers – I have learned so much from you.

A big shout-out to everyone in the village who has shown me support and encouragement – you know who you are!

A special thank-you to my mum, Leoni, who has read endless drafts of my work over the years and who instilled a love of writing in me in the first place. I love you.

Finally, thank you to my partner, Andy. You have been a ray of sunshine in my life since you walked into it more than ten years ago. Thank you for believing in me, even when I didn't believe in myself. Like so many things, I couldn't have done it without you.